DRAGONS

AND

GOLEMS

by
Eric Carlton Neperud

For Stanley,
Father and Olympic Athlete

By Eric Carlton Neperud

THE LIMBO CHRONICLES
>   Trees And Weeds
>   Limbo
>   The Octagonal Knight
>   Dragons And Golems
>   The Brotherhood Of Giants
>   Wizards And Druids

THE YELLOWSONE TRILOGY
>   Wonders Of The Wilderness
>   Fleas Upon Snow
>   The Periphery Of Sorrow

Copyright © 2017 by Eric Carlton Neperud
All rights reserved.
ISBN: 099838383X
ISBN-13: 978-0-9983838-3-5
Published by Valhalla Books

Cover Illustration by Eric Carlton Neperud
Map on back cover by Eric Carlton Neperud
Map on page 201 by Eric Carlton Neperud

Let's get one thing straight. I didn't steal because I had to. I wasn't one of those destitute spawns of a five year old mother and a drug-addicted father, who left her after the five minutes they spent together in the alley behind the bar they met in 10 minutes earlier. I stole because of the challenge. Could I do it? Would I ever get caught? The answers to both: yes. The latter, the progeny of a bloated hubris. Perfection, be it physical or intellectual, must have its blemishes. Without beauty marks and fatal flaws there is no baseline for comparison. Without experiencing sorrow one can't appreciate happiness. I believed I was infallible, so infallible I no longer disguised myself. Who would have thought a dishwasher that couldn't speak Esperanto would remember me? If he hadn't bussed that empty table at that moment I would still be free.

My life wasn't over. It was just changing. The part I didn't appreciate was my lack of input in that change. Most people dreaded being sentenced to a penal colony. It was a new opportunity for me. It wasn't that I didn't know if I was to survive. The uncertainty came in not knowing how long it would take and in what form. Joining a populace formed from incarceration was a dream gig. Criminals were generally less intelligent and less educated than the general population. I'll be the stone thrown at their glass house, the pawn completing its crossing of the board, the alligator in the pond of goldfish.

Chapter 1

NAKED

I walked naked haughtily through the transport portal. Their excuse was a lessening of contamination. Mine, a symbolic gesture of a new beginning. But how many infants have the intellect of a genius?

I stepped onto an irregular stone outcropping. An ordinary person would have stumbled, and possibly fallen, but I was always prepared for trouble, so a slight adjustment in each foot and knee is all I needed to remain upright. I glanced behind, already knowing what I would see. A wasted effort? Not when there was the possibility of something going amiss. One's misfortune was another's unexpected windfall. I've profited greatly from the axiom. No luck. The transport portal was gone. Would the people who designed this vast prison planet be that careless, to allow a two-way transport? Unlikely, but they weren't the ones guarding it.

I stood on a ridge: stone thrust through the backs of a queue of grassy knolls that became more prominent in the direction I faced. Behind me they gradually melted into the plain below. Being more comfortable with an ordered environment, I designated the rising of the ridge, the direction of the sun, as north. Yes, I know that was assuming I was in the southern hemisphere and it was noon. So many ifs and false interpretations. Being comfortable in my environment was more important than being accurate.

I'm here. Now what? I'm so isolated. I expected a processing center with hundreds of people clustered around. I can persuade people to do almost anything for me, but this rock, it can't even bring me a glass of water. I had to find a town. Should I follow the ridge up or down? Or veer off it, dropping down to that plain. No, that was too exposed. If a group of marauders rushed me I might not have enough time to convince them I must be their leader before they killed me. The higher I got the better my view. It would be best to survey this world's version of civilization from a distance.

Travel was easier than anticipated. The incline was gradual. I followed animal tracks whenever I could, the grass in many places being more than waist-high. During those occasions when wading became more prevalent than walking I climbed onto the rocky ridge.

I heard water running below me, apparently created from the ridge's runoff. I hadn't seen any lakes yet, or patches of snow, so the water must have been left over from the last rainstorm. Some of it still hadn't trickled down to the base of the mountains. I searched for the creek. Eventually finding the narrow stream, I drank my fill, then followed it. People couldn't survive without water, so if a settlement didn't appear along the stream's banks, it would certainly appear beside the larger body of water it fed. Yes, I had given up on following the ridge already, after just an hour. The view wasn't that good up here. And how likely was it that I would find someone living on top of a mountain?

As I carefully placed my feet along the rocky bank of the switchback creek, I pondered the remarkable coincidence that the northern end of the ridge was always in the direction of the sun. The range must have gradually veered to the west, but it looked straight to me. Eyes can be deceived, and I have used that to my advantage on numerous occasions. Maybe the refraction of light was different here. Terraforming sometimes created anomalies.

I was in the middle of my descent when it began to get dark. Dusk's arrived was unexpected. Sometimes it got dark quickly in the mountains, after the sun fell behind a peak. That's what must have happened. The orb finally had outpaced the ridge, falling to the right of it as I dropped to the left. That meant, on this planet, the sun set in the east. Equally likely, I was in the northern hemisphere, instead of the southern---but that meant refuting my hypothesis.

I was eager to complete my journey to the town that had to be just around the next bend in the creek, but was cognizant that hiking in the dark, particularly downhill, was treacherous, so I found a rocky shelf away from the waterway and lay beneath it---a precaution. Animals also required water, including predators.

It wasn't my thirst that drew me back to the stream, but the stench my arduous journey had created. I forced my tired, aching body up, walked back to the creek, then washed myself the best I could. I still probably had some of my scent on me. Hopefully not strong enough to attract something dangerous.

The cliché TOO TIRED TO SLEEP seemed to apply to me this evening. I knew I had to get some rest. The lethargy that would set in tomorrow would diminish my ability to travel and to defend myself, and more importantly, my ability to think my way out of undesirable situations. I had complete confidence in my ability to solve any problem, mundane or deadly---as long as I was in good health. That included having a robust mental alacrity.

Back to falling asleep. I used my foolproof method. I counted the money I received during my last JOURNEY OF CHILDREN. The beginning of every metric year, children travel from home to home after dark to collect a coin or two from each adult. It was a symbolic way to show the community cared for all of its children. Houses and streets were lit in bright lights and decorations. Because the Journey of Children could fall in any season, each celebration was unique. A child was prohibited from participating after he turned four. The time between Journeys was an eternity to most children. I was more aware of the bounty a child loses when he becomes an adult. Greater freedom didn't fully compensate for the loss of freebies. I was barely eligible the last time I participated. I considered it divine intervention that I was one of the largest, strongest and fastest walking the streets. I began the moment the sun passed below the horizon, the colors of the sky a precursor of the brilliance of the contents of my bucket at the end of the evening. As tradition dictated, the plastic, metal, porcelain, and wooden containers were in the shapes of animals. The poorer kids drew crude images on wash buckets. My family wasn't wealthy, but it had enough money to do what they wished with it. My bucket was in the shape of a shark, its upraised picket incisors enveloping the aperture. I was forced to re-use my bucket, year after year, my parents being admirably responsible with their money. I didn't mind. Appearance was just one tool. It could work against one as easily as for. After canvassing my neighborhood, I used city transport to travel to the most heavily populated areas of the city. At midnight the Journey of Children was officially over, but most houses turn off their lights an hour earlier. Every year fewer people retain the festive spirit. By the time I returned home I could barely move, not from fatigue, but from the weight of the coins I carried. Each time my bucket became full I emptied it into one of the bags slung over my shoulders. I knew my final Journey would be successful when one of the first houses I visited left a bowl full of coins in front of it. Either the owners were not home, or too lazy to answer the door. Most kids would have taken one coin and left the rest for other children. Obligation? Guilt? I dumped the contents of the bowl into my shark's mouth. It would be disrespectful to not take advantage of the opportunity. Being so close to home it was rational to return to deposit my initial collections. But only a spineless weakling was incapable of carrying all his money. If I couldn't carry it all, I didn't deserve to keep it.

FEEK! I had gotten off task---and hated myself for it. I don't mind people criticizing me. I just ignore them. I'm a much harsher critic of myself than they'll ever be. Not only was I not putting myself to sleep, I was working myself into a frenzy. Ah, childhood memories. I returned to the accomplishment of my goal. I began to mentally count the money I collected that evening. The task was so monotonous and the number so great it always put me to sleep.

Chapter 2

GROTTO

I awoke refreshed, but hungry. I needed to find some people who needed their food to be liberated. Living off the land wasn't beneath me, but I considered it a last resort. The area I was in was desolate. It would be a chore, without guarantee. Not the type of activity I usually participated in. Uncertainty to me was in quantity, not possibility.

Looking down I was reminded that food wasn't the only thing I hungered for. Why couldn't there be more female criminals? It would be more difficult, but no famine. I would be more desirable than the dim-witted brutes who were stupid enough to get caught.

I drank my fill at the creek. I was careful not to drink too quickly or too much. I didn't want to make myself sick. I returned to my abandonment of the mountains. An opening through boulders revealed I was more than halfway down. By midday I ought to be stepping onto plains.

My feet began to ache. Being as proud of my body as my intellect I didn't shun nudity, but there were reasons other than modesty one wore clothing. The blisters I developed began to pop on the jagged rocks I couldn't entirely circumvent. Painful initially, then tabs to rip flesh. I had to find something to replace the skin I lost, and to alleviate further deterioration of my feet.

Using bark stripped from cottonwoods and entwined straw grass I made a pair of rudimentary moccasins. I padded them with tufts of cotton. It was still painful to walk, but less so, and most importantly, I did no additional damage to my feet.

The creek made its plunge onto the plain at the base of the mountains as a modest waterfall. The water pooled beneath it, then meandered through the lush, tall grass that turned golden and sparse as the moisture from the misting falls became a memory.

Near the falls a trail paralleled the range. It traveled in both directions as far as my sight permitted. It crossed the creek at a ford. Footprints in the muddy descent to the ford revealed I wasn't the only person who had walked barefoot on this planet. There were also boot prints. So, industry had developed on Dartmoor (the name given to the penal colony). But to what degree, and how widespread?

What had it been like those first few years after the planet had been inhabited? And more importantly, what will it be like years from now? Dartmoor was still in its early stages. I could still mold it into whatever I wanted.

I elected to settle beside the falls, for the time being. The road nearby would eventually bring people to me. Why should I do any unnecessary traveling if I didn't have to?

The only creatures I saw the remainder of the day, human or non, were birds and lizards, the latter sunning themselves on the rocks above the falls. I named the creek after them. I called the single-groove trail the Tarsal Highway, it being at the base of the foothills.

After eating two handfuls of blackberries I had collected beside the grotto beneath the falls, I searched for a cave I could use for shelter until I could coerce someone into building a home for me. The berries gave me a burst of energy, but they weren't going to sustain me for the duration. I needed some protein soon, before its absence began to erode my abilities. Brawn would suffer the most, initially, but I was more concerned with my wits. If I had degenerated into a bumbling idiot by the time I met someone I would be at their mercy instead of theirs at mine. The grotto pool percolated with fish. Sometime, soon, I was going to have to figure out those steps between pond and market.

I found half-a-dozen caves. Some were too shallow. Some too deep. I wanted the opening to be large enough to transmit sufficient illumination, but not too large that it exposed the cave to the elements. The cave I settled on had a horizontal opening. On winter days when the sun was low it would allow in the maximum amount of light, and in the summer, when the sun was the highest, nearly none at all. The cave went back far enough that wind and rain shouldn't be a problem.

I made numerous trips to the edge of the prairie to transport armfuls of the straw-grass into the deepest part of the cave, where I intended to sleep. If I piled the vegetation high enough my body wouldn't notice I was sleeping on stone.

I ate another two handfuls of berries---outside the cave. I was very aware that I shouldn't contaminate my residence with anything edible, at least until I sealed my sleeping quarters. Uninvited bed buddies in the wild were less enjoyable than those portrayed in holographs.

When it became dark it became very dark, the grotto already concealed in shadow. Not being able to accomplish much in the dark, I went to bed after relieving myself outside the cave. Men with an overabundance of testosterone might choose to mark their territory. I considered the entire universe my own. Now, that would require a lot of urine. No, I was too fastidious, too organized, to scatter my refuse among my bedding.

After having relations with a woman I sleep alone. To distinguish the two activities I have separate bedrooms. I'm a perfect gentleman. She's permitted to remain in the initial bed the remainder of the night. If I am particularly enamored with her I might even return to her after I wake.

Chapter 3

CARAVAN

I heard many sounds that night, some in my cave, but nothing bothered me, not directly. Eventually I fell asleep, and just minutes later, or so it seemed, it was light. It was said that having a low intelligence was a gift, because a man with limited wit seldom pondered. His world was simple and happy. My world wasn't. How was I to catch fish? How was I going to make my shelter more livable? How was I to manufacture clothing? How long would it be until someone traveled past Lizard Spring (what I named my future settlement)? What would I say to them? What would I have them do for me first? What could I trade with other settlements to prosper my own? Would I one day have a serious relationship with one of the few women on Dartmoor? An incarcerated woman? Women were too much trouble.

If I was to survive I needed assistance. If I was going to meet people I had to monitor the Tarsal Highway. There could have been a group or two that passed me already, while I was in the grotto. The water from the falls was loud enough to block out anything short of a traveling carnival. My plan consisted of two parts. One, return to the road every hour. And two, put some kind of sign up at the Lizard Creek ford. Cottonwood bark would do, with words written in blackberry juice. It had to be short and simple: COLD WATER. I also drew an arrow pointing towards the grotto.

Between perusals of the Tarsal Highway I began OPERATION FISHING. With so many fish visible through the crystal waters of the grotto pool I thought it would be simple enough to just spear them. I sharpened the sturdiest, straightest, longest stick I could find, on a stone. Confident in my pre-determined success, I casually threw the spear towards a fish. The fish wasn't close to being skewered, and my spear was lost. After constructing another spear, I returned to the task, with more caution. I stabbed with the weapon instead of throwing it, careful to not lose physical contact with it. Every perfect thrust miraculously missed. How could the fish be so lucky? As I lifted my spear out of the water for the tenth time, I became aware of my mistake. The spear bent at the boundary between liquid and air. Of course. It was rudimentary physics. The refraction of light was different in different mediums. I had to compensate for the optical illusion. Still no success. The fish weren't even startled from my murderous attempts. They didn't scatter. I became upset and threw a rock at them. The rock took much longer to reach them than it should have. The fish scattered this time. Seconds later the pebble settled to the bottom of the pool. The water had to be deeper, much deeper, than my presumption. I was accustomed to polluted, technological worlds. Dartmoor was pristine. To see the bottom of a pool at home meant it was less than a meter deep. How far down could a person see in clear water? Two meters? Three? Five? Ten?

I needed to construct fishing line and a hook. I twisted blades of grass together. The line wouldn't last the day, but maybe until I caught something, especially if I doubled or tripled it. For the hook, I whittled a piece of wood. For bait? Blackberries. I delicately skewered three berries on the irregular barbs, then whipped the line towards the water. One of the berries came off. The other two bobbed on the surface of the pool. The hook needed to be heavier. I tied pebbles to the end of the line. After replacing the lost berry, I flung the line back out. This time two berries fell off, presumably the two that were water logged. The third berry was pulled towards the bottom of the pool. The fish were initially frightened of my contraption, then fascinated, but they never actually bit into the remaining berry. There was a reason you never read about fishermen using vegetables or fruit for bait.

I gave up, for the day. I checked the Tarsal Highway one more time. I had only been on Dartmoor for three days, but already

I felt my physical and mental faculties diminishing. I was determined to remain beside the road until dark.

An hour or so later I actually did see something. At first I believed it to be wishful thinking, my psyche creating an optical illusion. Or a mirage. The caravan was coming from the north. There were at least three people. They glowed brightly under a sun that never seemed to move.

Living on a world with a stationary sun did bother me, but with just trying to survive, I didn't put too much effort into understanding an anomaly that was unlikely to harm me. It did get dark every day. Now, that would get exhausting, trying to fall asleep in the middle of a perpetual day. But no, the sun eventually disappeared. Instead of falling below the horizon it turned off. Not completely. It dimmed, illuminated the night as brightly as a full moon.

The orb must have reflected off something they carried or wore that was metallic. In the state of mind I was in I was compelled to run towards them. Compelled, but not carried away. My senses were not completely shot. I waited on my side of the ford, but watching them earnestly. There was something in the sky: three objects. They were coming from the prairie. They were the size of eagles, but their wing structure was all wrong. They hovered more than soared. They were stout, much thicker of torso than birds usually were. As they came closer to both me and the caravan their features became more distinct. They were insects, not birds, monstrous in size. Terraforming has caused mutations, but nothing this extreme.

The caravan finally noticed the flyers. It stopped, still about 500 meters from the ford. The reflecting metal appeared to be armor. It must have been exceedingly broad, because it made its wearers appear almost squat.

The flyers were almost to the caravan now. In the manner the shiny men reacted to them, the encounter wasn't welcomed. They dropped their large packs---nearly as large as themselves---on the ground. They detached what looked to be crossbows from the packs. The men waited until the flyers were almost upon them to fire. The flyers flawlessly dodged the bolts, even at near point blank range.

I was wrong about the size of the flyers. They were larger than eagles, at least three times as large as the men. Before the men could exchange their crossbows for something more suitable for close range, they were swooped up one by one by the flyers. The men thrashed about madly, kicking and punching. Before the pounding could accumulate into a lost grip, the flyers bit off the flaying limbs, midair, then the heads. When all that was left was the armor---and what was left of the men inside---the bodies were dropped. They landed hundreds of meters to the left of the Tarsal Highway.

I debated whether to run towards the bodies or to flee to the safety of my cave. I ended up doing neither. I stared ahead, in shock, until dusk.

I rushed back to my cave. There was enough moonlight to make my way to the grotto, but just barely. The walls of the horseshoe valley were steep enough that trivial direct light illuminated it. I didn't sleep well. For the first time in my adult life I was unsure of myself.

Chapter 4

GOLD

Curiosity (of what might be in the discarded packs) superseded apprehension (of the flyers returning). After another unsatisfying breakfast of blackberries and creek water, I warily trudged to the packs. They were still in the middle of the Tarsal

Highway. No flyers---yet.

Crossbows and axes were scattered among the three packs that looked larger the day before. They were barely 100 sims tall. I picked up one. It was just as heavy as I imaged it to be. One was all I could carry, in my dilapidated state. To make the minimum number of trips I attached a crossbow and an axe to each pack. It made them heavier, but manageable, if I stopped every 50 meters or so to rest. I was tempted to search the packs immediately, but that meant exposing myself longer. No, it wasn't necessary to pick and choose. Everything in the packs would be used, eventually. When you carried your possessions on your back everything served a function.

As I returned for the third pack, I noticed vultures pecking at something to the left of the Tarsal Highway. I don't know why I did it. Was it a noble gesture? A final attempt at defending another's dignity? More likely, four days of built up frustration.

I took the crossbow and the axe from the remaining pack, and with careless determination, marched towards the vultures. I loaded one of the five bolts I had found into the crossbow. It surprised me too, how competent I was. When I felt I was within range I set down the other bolts and the axe, then fired at one of the birds. I was as stunned as it when the bolt hit its mark. How was I able to hit something that far away with a weapon I never used, but couldn't skewer something with a stick at point blank range? The other scavengers appeared to be more confused than mad or frightened. I loaded a second bolt. It too met its mark. The birds flew away this time. Probably not permanently, but it did provide the time I needed to give what was left of the men a proper burial.

The stench was bad, but it would be much worse in another day or two. I intended to bury the torsos as is, but changed my mind after identifying the value of the armor. With emotional abandonment, I stripped them of their armor and buried what was beneath in one large pit. Seeing up close what remained of the men, I now understood why the packs originally looked bigger. The men were pygmies, less than 150 sims tall---what I estimated them to be if their heads and legs were still attached to their torsos. And there was a reason the armor was extra wide: the men were extra wide. A mutation? But hereditary or environmental?

I carried the armor back to my cave, then the final pack with the crossbow and axe reattached. I made one more trip into the prairie to drag the oversize vulture carcasses to the grotto. If I could build a fire before the poultry spoiled I'll be living well for a few days, maybe even weeks if I could preserve the meat by smoking or salting it.

Back safely in my cave I studied the contents of the three packs. They consisted primarily of camping provisions: tents, bedrolls, water, dried meat---and dehydrated mushrooms. One of the packs had a map drawn on a hide. Within a circle were mountains, forests, rivers, and seas. Cities were also indicated. The center of the circle was represented by a blazing orb. A mountain range lay a sim to the right of it. I was fascinated by the map. If I could pinpoint where I was, it would become my birth certificate.

Returning to the pack, I found a flint, a lantern, and flasks of oil. I now had light at night and a method to start a fire. Clothes filled the remainder of the pack. The trousers, shirts, and undergarments were big enough around, but short. I put them on, having to cinch the trousers. I was quite a sight, with my stomach and a third of my legs exposed. I also found a pair of stockings, but no boots. The stockings were heavier than they should have been. I felt inside: stones? I poured them out and found...GOLD NUGGETS! I meticulously searched the other two packs. They also contained gold. Combined, I had a pile that weighed...maybe a kilo. With a bit of seed money success was now guaranteed.

I put the gold and the map into a leather bag I found in one of the packs. I hid it in a cavity near the rear of the cave, then concealed it with a larger stone. I was the only person within kays of the grotto, but that could change any moment, if I was lucky.

Next up: preserving the fowl. I piled stones in two heaps in one of the smaller caves. I found a sturdy, long stick and skewered the vultures. I placed the ends of the pole on top of two stacks of stones I constructed, adding an extra layer of rocks on top to steady the contraption. I built a fire beneath the fowl. Smoke rapidly filled the small, semi-enclosed area. I coughed as I fled. Every ten minutes I returned to the cave to turn the pole a quarter turn. I wasn't sure how long to cook/smoke the birds, but I'd rather overcook the meat than undercook it. My intention was to alternate turning the pole with watching the Tarsal Highway. An hour between sightings had been too long. A handful of groups could have passed Lizard Spring already, sight unseen. I hated to admit it, but I believe I was becoming lonely.

Chapter 5

OBSIDIAN

Early in life (pre-adolescence), I challenged myself to learn something every day. Today I learned that tunnel vision, a useful tool for focused concentration, had its detriments. Someone had entered the grotto without me instantly noticing him. He was just 20 meters away. He was taller than me, as were most men. The size, or shape, of one's body wasn't important. It was what you did with it. His hair was blond, more golden than platinum. His skin was bronze, like he had spent most of his time outdoors. His clothes were white, looking like they were woven from cotton. He wore sandals. They also appeared to be constructed from cotton. His eyes were brown, but of a light hue, making them appear nearly the same shade as his skin. He was muscular, but not in an exaggerated manner: more toned, than body-built. If one compared the two of us, I was the before hologram and he was the after.

17

"I noticed your smoke," he spoke to me in a deep, even-toned voice. I looked stupidly at the rising billow. How could he not?

In a whiny, high-pitched, stuttering voice I answered back, "Would you like to join me for dinner?"

"I'm a vegetarian, of sorts. I eat fish. If you don't mind me catching a couple in your pond, we can share a table."

By the time I had hacked away enough of one of the birds for a meal, dusk had arrived. The bronze man was filleting a fish. How did he catch it? He didn't have a fishing pole or a net. "I don't have a pan," I said to him as I headed towards my cave.

"I eat my fish raw. I'll join you in a couple of minutes."

I lit the lantern. Immediately, a cloud of insects swarmed it. Dark, elongated shapes danced on the cave walls.

The bronze man entered. "We can lean against the packs," I told him.

As I chewed the buzzard with much vigor, the bronze man delicately bit into the pale-pink fish flesh like he was biting into a flaky pastry.

"I would be wary who I showed those packs to," spoke the bronze man between bites. "You have salvage rights, but troglodytes are possessive of their own, especially their gold. They might forgive an infant, but that is a mighty iffy might."

"Troglodytes? Cave men?"

"Cave dwellers."

"There was something odd about them. They weren't just short. Their features looked contorted, like someone had squished them."

"I'm not sure they would find humor in the description. Then again, trogs don't find humor in most things. They are stoic, as are most who dwell in Orpo."

I attempted to connect the name to a place on the map I found. I couldn't. That didn't mean it wasn't there---I didn't have a photographic memory---just unlikely. There was going to be a lot to learn. I didn't mind doing that, as long as I was actually learning something. I usually knew more than my teachers. That got me into trouble at first, before I realized that being kicked out of school wasn't going to advance my career. It was easier to win the game if one knew the rules.

"Stoic, huh?" I was already attempting to assess how valuable these troglodytes might be to me. Stoic usually meant hard-working, and rarely complaining. Perfect for semi-skilled labor. "So where exactly is this Orpo?"

The bronze man began to laugh. I never liked laughing. I always thought it to be so...uncivilized. When I was younger I believed it to be directed at me, even when the person doing the laughing wasn't facing me. Every comment, every question someone asked, had to somehow be connected to me. As I got older I no longer cared.

"Oh, Nimbus, we are no longer in Kansas."

Another place that wasn't on the map. "Is IT nearby?"

The bronze man laughed again. I wanted to pound his skull in, but I didn't. Civilized people didn't do that. I was gifted in keeping myself under control. Be it 40 degrees or minus 40, I was able to remain motionless, for hours. After getting severely burned, and frostbit, I recognized there were peripheral consequences to my stubbornness, but I did make my point.

"It's just an idiom. What now, Nimbus?"

"What now? I'm going to bed. This would be about the time I would politely ask you to leave, and close the door behind you. Since I don't have a door all I can do is the polite asking. Why do you continue to call me Nimbus? It sounds like you're trying to insult me?"

"I call you, Nimbus, because that is your name. By the way, my name is Obsidian, Obsidian Central Forest."

"Now, that's a mouthful. You must have me confused with someone else. Even if I thought less of myself I would never name myself after a cloud." Actually, I kind of liked the name: to loft high in the sky looking down on others.

"It's tradition for new arrivals to be named by someone who has been here longer."

19

"And how long is that."

"Significantly longer in my case."

Obsidian wasn't a kid, but he wasn't an old man either. Not even middle-aged. Less than ten. Maybe as young as eight. I haven't heard of adolescents being sent to Dartmoor. Anything was possible, with the public usually not being informed of controversial issues, adhering to their UNLESS YOU FIND OUT, WE WON'T TELL policy.

"So Nimbus Southern Spine it is," spoke the bronze man firmly, like he was giving a sentence.

"That's a bit awkward, isn't it?" I made peace with Nimbus already. I kind of liked the idea of starting over. That had to include my name. The last part of my name was obviously in reference to the mountain range I climbed off of.

"You'll get used to it, infant."

"If you're trying to upset me I've been called worse, a lot worse."

"All newcomers to Limbo are called infant. Think about it."

"Limbo? Is that what people call this part of Dartmoor?"

"It's what we call the entire planet. After a few years we no longer associate it with being a penal colony."

"How did you know I have gold?" I looked towards one of the axes. It could be in my hands in seconds.

"Don't worry. I don't want the gold. Money is just a tool. One of those axes is a better tool at this moment now anyway." I grabbed the axe. "I knew you had gold, because trogs always have gold, and you clearly scavenged some of their possessions."

"I found them."

"Of course. I said you have salvage rights. An infant couldn't have possibly killed three dwarves."

"Isn't that politically incorrect, calling them dwarves?"

"Do you think someone earning a life sentence cares what other people think? I called them dwarves because that is what they used to be called, before troglodyte was determined to be less offensive. Sometimes I lose track of time, getting one era confused with another."

"You talk like you're 25 years old."

The bronze man laughed. "I wish I was 25 again. No, I don't. You don't really learn who you are until you're at least 50."

"How is that possible? Even if you looked the part, people just don't live that long."

"They do on Limbo. Longer."

"How long?"

"We may never know. Indefinitely perhaps. No one has died yet to refute the theory."

"So you're saying once we step onto Dartmoor...ah Limbo...soil we become immortal?"

"Haven't you wondered why we call this place what we do? This immortality thing isn't instantaneous. It doesn't take effect until we die."

"Isn't that contradictory?"

"Obviously, we don't really die. Not completely. Our body may expire, but our soul lingers. Before it can escape it's enveloped by a new body."

"The same body, fully grown?"

"Fully grown, but not always the same. In its successful attempt to save us, Limbo changes us."

"So we mutate." Like those monstrous insects.

"Not all mutations are detrimental. Most are open to interpretation, to what is beneficial and what isn't. Most aren't severe enough to be noticed."

"But some are. The trogs, for instance."

"Yes, but even with them, the changes weren't instantaneous. Psychological alterations usually proceed physical ones, multiple mutations following multiple deaths."

"Near deaths."

"Yes."

"So when we were given a life sentence, the judge wasn't joking?"

"It has to do with the creation matrix that terraformed this planet."

"So, I'm going to change into a trog one day?"

"Or something entirely different. Mutations vary in diversity and severity. There is a way out of it: don't die."

"So, if I'm cautious, I may not mutate?"

"IF is the definitive word. Limbo does what it can expedite the process. Most infants die within the first year. It's rare to see someone with gray hair who didn't arrive with it."

"So there really isn't any hope?"

"Not for the long run. But one's life can be extended if he lives in a city. Mutual protection is a wonderful thing. Very few humans attack one another anymore. It's called the HUMAN PACT. There are more than enough confrontation opportunities outside human settlements."

"How far away is the closest city?"

"Wayward Gull is 74 kays south of here. I don't think I would call it a city. It barely has 200 souls."

"Is that enough people to defend against a pack of mutants?"

"Very few groups of mutants are in numbers large enough to form packs yet, or herds, or flocks, but when they do I'm confident settlements will have also increased their populations."

"What population do you think a city needs for it to be able to adequately defend itself against mutants?"

"It depends on its location. Central Limbo is much safer than the Frontier, where the most extreme mutants live. Here, a population of 40 or 50 should be sufficient to deter most confrontations."

"Then I have a proposition to discuss with you."

Chapter 6

LIZARD FALLS

Through an entire flask of oil we discussed the creation of Lizard Falls. My learning curve would be substantially smaller with Obsidian's help. What did Obsidian get out of our partnership? Entertainment, at least that is how I perceived it. He was a nomad, a wanderer. He paused along his perpetual journey only long enough to pique his curiosity. When he got tired of me and my project he would leave, which made it better for me---and him. I didn't like to share power, and eventually my push for control would get messy.

The grotto held a natural defensive position. All we had to do once we established a minimal population was to fence in the lower end of the small, deep valley, which I called Sushi Cove, after my partner's eating habits. There was also the possibility of attack from atop the falls, so it would also have to be fenced in, eventually. The administrative offices would be in the cove, as would emergency survival residences. The town would expand towards the Tarsal Highway. In time, the outer settlement would be walled in like the cove, assuming there was enough of a population to warrant it.

It didn't take long for our first residents to arrive. The sign at the ford announcing cool, fresh water did what it was intended to do. A weary caravan entered the cove looking for refreshment and a night's lodging. The group of five men and one woman had the coin to pay for as many rooms as I had available. They had come from Gulag, Limbo's largest settlement, and only bona fide city. It was experiencing rapid growth, encouraged by the construction of something called the WIZARD'S TOWER nearby.

Everyone didn't enjoy that much excitement. Other emigrants from the city of more than 10,000 would eventually pass through Lizard Falls. I needed to build a hotel immediately.

For a nominal fee we permitted the caravan to camp beside the grotto pool. From their interactions with one another I learned that they were more than just traveling companions. The unequal distribution of men to women created a shift in the social structure. Multiple-husband/one-wife marriages began to form. The confusion of whose husband fathered what child didn't occur because we were made sterile before our release on Limbo. Being the head of the household, it was the woman's duty to name her family. Feminine words were often used, flowers in particular. The Marigolds agreed to stay with us after enjoying the sweet cool, tangy water from a spring that flowed into the creek. The minerals in it gave everyone who drank from it an increase in energy. They also enjoyed listening to the soothing sounds of the waterfall. To cement the deal I offered them trog gold to build a hotel for me.

Before the construction was completed another two families had joined us, and a handful of singles. The Posies and the Foxgloves were as pleased to remove themselves from the commotion of the city as the Marigolds. The singles were frustrated with the faithfulness of the wives. The Foxgloves were willing to increase their family, accepting two of the bachelors. A majority of the remaining singles moved on, men not subsisting on gold alone.

I was the type of person that made someone's disadvantage my advantage. Prostitution was common in Limbo, but it was frowned upon in Gulag, the local religious sect, THE THIRD TIME IS A CHARM CHURCH, vehemently condemning it. Once the hotel was completed I could make a killing on room service. The difficulty was in acquiring employees willing to provide such service. The three women in Lizard Falls were all in committed relationships. Not only were women scarce, they also had the power in Limbo, at least over themselves. Demand exceeded supply. How many self-confident women were willing to sell their bodies? I needed to find professional, career-oriented women. It took a month after the hotel was built to find the first. Thank Gaea---what the locals called God---she came with three friends.

By this time cottages were being built outside the cove. Sanitation was becoming a problem. A group toilet was built within one of the cottages. Eventually a sewer system was created, but that was a year later. Bathing continued to occur in the pool until a bathhouse was constructed a month after the group toilet. Water was diverted from the creek using bamboo piping. The fence protecting the cove was also built at this time. We hadn't yet encountered any marauding mutants, but I would much rather build a fence I never needed than not build one and wish I had.

Food was becoming a problem. The pool was almost fished out, as was the creek. Hunting parties were established, with varying degrees of success. Farming was begun, begrudgingly. Criminals preferred killing things over digging in the ground.

The four professional women were members of the Prostitute Guild. They didn't consider themselves anyone's employees. They were contracted associates. They shared profits equally with the owners of the venues they worked in. Certain comfort and safety issues had to be met. An accounting of all monies collected had to be made every month. They also had the right to refuse service to any potential customer. At first I was put off by the Prostitute Guild's demands, but after more careful consideration I realized those guidelines were going to make their operation more self-sufficient, freeing up my time to work on new ventures.

A community couldn't survive on prostitution alone, so I had to create an industry. To make it successful I had to either do something better than anyone else, or produce something original, something that no one else produced. As with most of Lizard Falls' developments, Obsidian was crucial. "Why not sell our water? Everyone who drinks from the spring says it's the best they have tasted, and it invigorates them like a drug." That's how the LIZARD SPRINGS BOTTLING COMPANY was born.

The product was readily available---that wasn't the problem.

Bottling it and distributing it was a different story. Sand was readily available in the prairie to make glass, but the process was still time consuming. We opted for large glass barrels instead of small individual bottles. Wagons would carry the glass kegs to settlements. This was many years prior to the moral prohibition on beasts of burden, so although difficult to acquire, oxen were available for hauling. Once a substantial number of glass kegs were distributed into the global community full kegs could be exchanged for used ones, reducing costs for all. My cash cow was squirting milk.

As the Lizard Springs Bottling Company prospered, so did Lizard Falls. We were larger than Wayward Gull already and in the process of expanding across the Tarsal Highway. In another year or two our population would be great enough to support the construction of a city wall, which would establish us as a proper town, instead of just a village. The Grotto Inn was so popular that reservations had to be made. The local chapter of the Prostitute Guild built their own structure to headquarter the side businesses their enormous profits bought. I never learned all the products they sold, but most were exotic and rather expensive. The first floor showroom was so successful they had to hire a sales staff, they not having enough time themselves to sell their products.

As a fringe benefit of my accomplishments I met a lot of interesting people, from every corner of Limbo. I was fortunate to not arrive in the Frontier. I would have had to work hard just to stay alive.

Chapter 7

TREASURE HUNT

Of the many tales I heard the ones that stood out were about treasures, those lost, and those hoarded. Criminals were very fond of treasure. When they weren't attempting to collect it they were THINKING about collecting it, myself included. Because criminals didn't trust one another they usually carried their treasure with them. Living on Limbo made one death prone, so some of that treasure was left in unusual places. Some of the monsters---the mutants so mutated they no longer resembled humans---enjoyed the wealth they accumulated almost as much as they did before they were altered. Others gave up the lust when their humanity was taken from them. Either/or, the more powerful the monster, the larger it's treasure. Each successive human's failure of retrieving it made it grow larger.

One such large treasure was within the Southern Spine. Directions were inconsistent due to the sun never moving. North was arbitrarily put at one edge of a circle---incidentally, in the direction I had chosen for north---and south at the opposite edge. As the Lizard Creek Bottling Company expanded and my conversations with people accumulated, my map of Limbo became more relevant. I added Lizard Falls to it. The town was relatively close to the center of the known world: 200 kays, compared to a 1000 kay diameter.

Nothing lay beyond the frontier boundaries, not even hints. No one I talked to could tell me anything substantial. Some mentioned a negation of illumination at the edge of the world. Others mentioned an energy shield. A third group spoke of a cliff and a bottomless drop.

"You still plan to ransack Scree Castle?" asked Obsidian from my office. I had constructed it in the grotto cave I had used as my home these past three years. Although I had the resources to build a mansion I chose to remain where I was for sentimental reasons, after many modifications, of course. I had a real bed now, and water and sewage lines. A bluewood desk was placed near the entrance of the cave, beside a matching cushioned chair. Candles lit the cave instead of that smelly oil lantern. A safe full of gold was built into the back of the cave. A double set of doors provided environmental stability and safety. The interior one was constructed of glass, to allow light in. The exterior of metal, which I closed at night. No one could enter my cave if I didn't want them to, unless they were very determined and had the proper equipment.

"Scree Castle," I echoed. Obsidian was almost ready to leave me. The novelty must have finally wore off. I don't blame him. If I met someone like me I wouldn't want to hang around long either. Although I've looked forward to the day I'll be able to run Lizard Falls by myself, I would also miss him. Very few people I've met have had his intelligence and wisdom. A prison planet isn't the best place to meet people of quality. I've also known him since my first week on Limbo. He was more of a brother to me than an associate. Oh, well.

"Yes, Scree Castle," he repeated. "This venture will likely be your first failure. How do you propose collecting the treasure? Will Lord Scree conveniently fall on his sword? Will he just give it to you? Salvage rights don't apply to the living."

That was a bit harsh, especially coming from Obsidian. He was right, though. I don't know if it was my self-confidence, or my greed, but I ignored him and continued my plans to free Scree Castle of its treasure.

I didn't see Obsidian again until the morning I left for Scree Castle. Every month since I met him he would leave for two or three weeks. He always left in the early morning, before it became light. I once sent a couple of henchmen to follow him. Traveling in the dark was never a good idea on Limbo. Something large charged them. They ran back to Lizard Falls too frightened to look back at what attacked them.

The men I took with me were mercenaries. My own men had it too good to risk their lives. Nothing reduced one's drive like success. I didn't blame them. Men were weak. Mercenaries were a gamble, since they just had money riding on the mission, but they were trained, and blooded already. Their leader was Sergeant Stub. He retained all of his limbs---and digits---but that didn't mean he always did. Re-creations weren't always detrimental. He was fully bearded, as were most of the men on Limbo. The rest of him appeared to be just as hairy. Extra testosterone was expected with a military man. If he shaved his legs, then I would have worried. His company numbered an even score. They wore studded leather armor and metal helmets. Each had a bow, a quiver of arrows, and a shield strapped to his backpack. And a sword and dagger embedded in scabbards.

Obsidian intercepted us as we passed through the grotto gate. "I believe this endeavor to be foolish, but I do offer you some advice to increase your opportunity for success, if you choose to take it."

"By all means. You haven't given me bad advice yet, except possibly in your overly cautious attitude about Scree Castle."

"Your only hope for success is entering the castle unnoticed."

"You must have a means to make us invisible, then," said Sergeant Stub, "because that is the only way we are entering Scree Castle without Lord Scree becoming aware of it."

"Maybe we could use a sleeping elixir," suggested Corporal Pear. "Do you remember the kob camp we massacred a year-and-a-half ago?"

"That was outdoors, where the gas could disperse rapidly. I don't believe enough of the guards in Scree Castle would be affected to prevent us from becoming crossbow pincushions."

"You don't have to go through the gate," said Obsidian. "There is a secret route beneath the castle, an escape tunnel."

"And you know where this secret entrance is?" I asked.

"It's in Bramble Valley."

"The only way into Bramble Valley is over Below Zero Ridge," stated Corporal Pear.

"The last I heard no one has successfully crossed it," said Sergeant Stub.

"Then how does anyone know about Bramble Valley?" I asked.

"The two people who saw the valley from the far side of the ridge died. After being re-created they told their tale."

"And they haven't returned?"

"They were too frightened."

"Is there no way a frontal attack can be successful?" I pleaded.

"There is always a way," said Obsidian, "but the cost to hire such an army would be prohibitive, perhaps as much as the value of the treasure. You still want to plunder Scree Castle?"

"Sergeant, are you still willing?" I asked him.

"Seeing that the likelihood of us ever collecting our pay is decreasing by the minute I believe a doubling of our share is appropriate."

"Is the money that important to you that you'll risk probable death?" asked Obsidian.

Trooper Moth responded. "This is our livelihood. We can't back down whenever we encounter a difficult opponent. This is our playoffs. Our lives are meaningful now. Robbing old women wasn't very noble. This is our opportunity to make amends."

"Important enough to risk mutation?"

"One of the characteristics of a mercenary is his high-tolerance for mutation," Corporal Pear explained. "Most of these men have died a handful of times and haven't noticeably mutated."

"I guess I will see you all after you have been re-created," said Obsidian. "May Negativity not seek you."

Chapter 8

CLIMBING

The trip up the Southern Spine was much more arduous than the trip down three years ago. We had to make camp twice before reaching the base of Below Zero Ridge.

The only event meriting a retelling was our encounter with four horned lizards the size of small whales. We preferred to detour around them, but they persisted in blocking our way. Corporal Pear released a warning arrow in hopes it would frighten them away. After it clunked against a rock the lizards slowly turned towards it, then apathetically turned their heads back in our direction.

Sergeant Stub looked at me. "I hate to waste so many arrows on them. Afterwards we'll have to collect as many of the undamaged ones as we can find." He turned to his troops. "Squads target an individual lizard. At my signal we'll fire instantaneously."

"You heard the boss," said Corporal Pear. "Alpha, target the lizard on the far left. Beta...."

"FIRE!"

Twenty arrows flew in unison. Only two missed their mark. Both happened to be targeting the same lizard. The eight meter long monstrosity scuttled towards its attackers. With surprising agility it captured one of the mercenaries in its jaws. After two quick adjustments of its mouth the man was swallowed whole.

A second wave of arrows finished off the critically injured lizards. The four men not firing threw down their bows and lunged towards the attacking lizard with swords drawn. They would have been more successful if they weren't so cautious in penetrating the lizard. There was still hope their comrade within could be saved.

They concentrated on the lizard's head. Its other end, not given any attention at all, whipped around and knocked two of the men off their feet. One of them hit his head and didn't get back up. Sergeant Stub and the men firing the second volley joined the melee. With the lizard being completely flanked, it was hastily destroyed, without additional injuries.

The swallowed mercenary was carefully cut out of the lizard's gut. He smelled horrendous. The digestive juices had already begun to dissolve his skin. He looked like he had second degree burns over his entire body. An ointment was applied to his skin. It instantly reduced the redness and swelling.

The mercenary who hit his head wasn't as fortunate. After his possessions were stripped off him his body was left to rot in the sun.

"Shouldn't we bury him or something?" I asked.

"Life has lost much of its dignity and sacredness on Limbo," Sergeant Pear explained. "If a person is to be re-created into a fresh, new body, why should we give his old body so much attention?"

"How about returning his possessions when he returns?"

"We don't always find a person after he is re-created. Re-creation locations are dependent on the morality of those that die, and the will of Gaea. If Trooper Walnut's psyche hasn't changed since his last re-creation he'll return about where he did last time. Mercenaries must retain a certain distance from what they do, so they are less likely to be modified than most Limboans. They are usually re-created near Gulag, the center of Neutrality. If we survive this job, we'll return there to find him. If we don't survive, we'll all probably be re-created within 20 kays or so of one another."

"Will his possessions be returned to him then?"

"Some of them," Corporal Pear replied. "A mercenary troop is weakened if some of its members aren't properly armored. Of course getting oneself killed carelessly shouldn't be rewarded, so any non-essential possessions, such as gold, aren't returned.

Limboans without friends don't have anything returned to them. For them, re-creation is truly starting over."

We were within sight of Below Zero Ridge the second night we camped. It wasn't yet dark, but Sergeant Stub insisted it soon would be. Without clocks and the sun never setting I wondered how he could be so certain. But by the time we had completed setting up camp sundim was upon us. Without external time clocks the Limboans must have developed their internal ones.

I had trouble sleeping, my mind focusing on my potential death, and my seemingly impossible rebirth. The foreboding and exhilaration of an impending adventure were almost over. It was going to be REAL starting tomorrow. What would it be like to be mutated? Would the change be drastic? Would I wake-up and find myself a hairy monster? Or would it be more gradual, taking multiple re-creations, like the transformation to an adolescent before becoming an adult?

Waking was both a blessing and a curse. My mind was freed from the endless loop, but I now had to face what had precipitated it.

I woke confused. It was still dark. The clanking of weapons and armor, and the boasting of impending victories permeating the air. Testosterone was flowing. Not just flowing, but bursting, like a dike that had been breached. After a light breakfast---who wants a heavy one before a long trek uphill---we resumed our climb.

In a zigzagging fashion we marched up the gray gravel and dust to the shimmering, milky white that seemed to be getting no closer. Each time we believed we were topping the ridge a shelf was reached instead. When we first hit snow our hope renewed. The snow was intermittent. The faux ridge tops continued.

We transitioned from a state of being overheated by our exertion to a state of being overcooled by the high-altitude. Snow was no longer just in the shadows.

"UP AHEAD!" Trooper Moth shouted. A dozen bighorn sheep looked down at us from the potential true summit.

"Do we attempt to circumvent them like the lizards?" I asked.

"We'll know in a minute or two," replied Sergeant Stub. "Proceed slowly, men. Stay close together. We want to occupy as little space as possible, to provide them plenty of escape routes if they become frightened."

The animals held their ground, but just briefly. We were obviously going to continue heading towards them, and we were more menacing than they were. They ran off, down the backside of the ridge.

Chapter 9

BELOW ZERO

Reaching the top of the ridge didn't mean instantaneous descent. Snowy mounds stretched as far as the eye could see. They were broken up intermittently by near vertical, rocky protrusions that varied from tens of meters tall to hundreds.

"We could easily be taken by surprise up here," said Corporal Pear. "There are too many places to hide."

"But surprised by whom?" asked Sergeant Stub. "Why would anything not adapted to this environment, like a mountain goat or a bighorn sheep, want to be up here?"

"What eats the sheep and goats?" asked Trooper Moth.

"Maybe nothing will attack a group as large as us," I said. "The sheep didn't want anything to do with us."

"The lizards did."

"We need to spread out so we can see in as many directions and angles as possible," said Sergeant Stub.

Corporal Pear echoed the orders, directing the troops.

"How long until we're off the ridge?" I asked.

"Preferably before sundim," replied Sergeant Stub. "The wind is already picking up. It feels like it's below zero already. Tonight will be unbearable up here."

We cautiously made our way towards where we thought Bramble Valley was. The sun's stationery location simplified orientation, but the sky had clouded over with the onset of the wind. We couldn't use our tracks any longer as guides, extending the vectors to sustain our course. They were being wind-blasted into oblivion behind us. It would have been prudent to set up camp and wait out the blizzard, if it wasn't for the likelihood of us freezing to death.

Someone screamed. It was beginning to snow, and with the wind, whiteout conditions had begun. I couldn't see more than five meters in any direction. Another voice screamed. "ALPHA, BETA, FIX!" spoke Corporal loudly.

"GAMMA, DELTA, ON ME!" spoke Sergeant Stub, just as loudly. I headed towards Sergeant Stub's voice. "GAMMA, DELTA, ON ME!" The bellow acted as a beacon. Sergeant Stub came into view. He looked serious, but un-frazzled. For the next few minutes the mercenary commander, nine troopers, and I, huddled together. I was on the verge of asking a question, but was immediately hushed. Sergeant Stub was focusing on listening.

"KILL IT!" shouted Corporal Pear's voice.

"IT WON'T LET ME GET CLOSE ENOUGH!" spoke another voice.

"MOTH IS DEAD!"

"SHOOT IT WITH YOUR CROSSBOW, THEN!"

"IT'S TOO FAR AWAY TO SEE!"

"KIWI IS ALSO DEAD!"

"I'LL KILL IT MYSELF!"

A moment later Corporal Pear screamed.

"ALL TROOPS FIX!" spoke Sergeant Stub curtly.

We rushed towards the other half of the troop. Trooper Moth was found first. He was a bloody pulp. The splattered blood in the snow looked like someone had dropped a cherry snow cone.

A few meters farther Trooper Kiwi was found in a similar state. Beyond him the remaining troopers surrounding Corporal Pear. He was still alive, for the moment. His skin was pale. He wasn't mauled like his companions. The white rubbery thing behind him was.

Corporal Pear closed his eyes. Sergeant Stub rushed to his side. He felt for a pulse. It was still there.

"It looked like a frog," said a trooper whose skin was almost as pale as Corporal Pear's. "It emitted an excruciating chill. Anyone coming within five meters of it was frost burned. The closer one got, the stronger the effect. Corporal Pear fought through the debilitating pain and skewered the creature."

"What happened to Moth and Kiwi?" asked Sergeant Stub.

"The frog also had sharp teeth."

"Some animals poison or paralyze their victims before eating them," I commented. "This FROG apparently freezes its prey."

"Is Corporal Pear going to recover?" asked the frostbit trooper.

Sergeant Stub studied his second-in-command more closely. The corporal's sword hand was turning black. "He's going to lose that arm, and I don't know what else. I hate to do it, but I think we're going to have to put him down."

"WAIT!" I bellowed.

"It'll be for the best. He'll be re-created near Gulag, fully healed."

"I have an idea. If I can possibly prevent a potential mutation, shouldn't I try?"

"A mercenary without his sword arm is no longer a mercenary."

"I believe I may be able to save it."

I extracted a flask of Lizard Spring Water from my pack and poured it on his arm. The blackness began to pale, like it was soaked in bleach. Its color continued to improve, eventually becoming the hue of healthy skin. I opened his mouth and poured a small amount down his throat. Then I gave him a bit more. The color in his face returned. A few minutes later he opened his eyes.

"I feel cold," he said.

"May I have some of that water?" asked the frostbit trooper. I gave him what remained in the bottle.

"That explains why people feel so revived after drinking Lizard Spring Water," said Sergeant Stub. "I believe you're going to become a wealthy man without stealing Lord Scree's treasure."

"Do you think we can revive Moth and Kiwi?" asked the no longer frostbit trooper.

"Dead is dead," I said. "After a tree dies, no matter how much water you give it, it won't recover. Sergeant Stub, you might want to reconsider setting up camp up here. My internal clock hasn't adjusted to Limboan time yet, but I don't think we're going to make it off the ridge before sundim."

"I think you're right."

"I've heard that snow is a great insulator. If we can burrow into it we'll stay above freezing tonight."

"Troopers to me. We got about an hour to dig a cave large enough for all of us. Let's head a hundred meters in that direction. That should put enough distance between us and these bodies. As an additional precaution, we'll bury the dead troopers and the frog. There are likely larger and more dangerous predators than this amphibian."

The snow cave was ready at sundim. After eating a cold meal we went to bed. I've heard of arctic aborigines building fires in igloos, the smoke exiting through a small hole, but the ridge was above the tree line, and we didn't bring any firewood. It was relatively warm in the cave, our body heat warming the air a few degrees above freezing. I was concerned our cave might melt. What did quickly refroze, reinforcing the structure with an icy layer.

We woke revived. The frostbit trooper was completely healed and Corporal Pear was well enough to travel. If we had any more Lizard Spring Water he may have been completely healed within another day, but I had brought just one flask with me.

The storm appeared to be over. There was still some wind,

as there probably always was on the ridge, but the sun was out, more than countering the wind chill.

It was turning into a pretty day, if it was possible for any day following the deaths of two people could be considered so. No longer having whiteout conditions, we now knew which direction to travel. We hadn't been completely turned around, but we weren't going to get ourselves off the ridge in the direction we were heading either.

The nice weather must have made us complacent, because one of the outlier troopers was snatched by a giant, clawed worm, and swallowed whole. Were all large creatures that lazy that they didn't take the time to chew before swallowing?

"Troopers," said Sergeant Stub. "Same procedure as we used for the lizard. We don't want to accidentally kill the man inside." The rescue attempt was more difficult. Not only was the creature twice as long, which meant eight times as large when extended in three dimensions, it had claws, two dozen of them. It raised its head, flaring the sides of its countenance like a cobra. It was as quick as one. It snatched two more troopers before it was struck. The sword making contact with the glowing-red back ridge melted. The trooper holding it exclaimed, more from surprise than from his hand being burnt. The momentary shock delayed our attack long enough for the frost worm to flip its head around and consume one more man.

"We need to change tactics," spoke Corporal Pear from the sidelines due to his injury. "We need to strike at its weakest point. It exposes its belly whenever it lifts its head."

"Aim for its belly," echoed Sergeant Stub.

The first trooper attempting the maneuver was shredded apart from the creature's claws. None of the pieces were big enough for the worm to bother with consuming. Corporal Pear couldn't take it anymore. With a sword in his offhand he charged the worm. He pierced its belly, then slid it through its flesh like he was opening a letter. The worm's last act was to bend down its neck and attempt to swallow the corporal. It was partially successful. The corporal flayed his exposed legs as the 15 meter long monstrosity fell on top of him.

Without delay Sergeant Stub and his troopers cut into the worm, attempting to free Corporal Pear and the other troopers. Being partially inside the worm lessened the impact of its bulk falling on the corporal. The part of him found inside the worm wasn't worth saving. His head and shoulders looked like a melted wax dummy. The heat that melted the sword must have continued into the interior of the worm. The troopers that had been consumed earlier were no longer recognizable as human.

Why were four men killed to unsuccessfully save one? If decisions were based on cost-benefit analysis the men wouldn't have died. But wouldn't I have wanted someone to attempt to save me? Could I allow a loved one to die a certain death? Humanity prevails. Once I am no longer human will I feel the same?

"May these men not mutate when they are re-created," spoke Sergeant Stub. We left them, and the worm, were they lay. At night, while we were stationary, it was beneficial for carnivores and scavengers not to be cognizant of carcasses, but during the day, it was better for predators to concentrate on an area, in exchange for not harassing us.

The green of Bramble Valley was a welcomed sight. More welcomed if we hadn't lost a third of our troop already.

A bramble is a thicket, an entangled brushy jungle. Traveling in such an environment wasn't fast, or easy. We were thoroughly scraped by the time we had traveled five kilometers, the duration of our daylight.

What a contrast sleeping that night was compared to the previous one. West of the Southern Spine the air had been relatively dry, corroborated by the lack of vegetation. Bramble Valley was warm and humid, almost suffocating, particularly in comparison to the breezy chill of Below Zero Ridge. It was not easy to sleep in the stale, steamy air. We kept a three person watch. It felt token considering what we had been though. Fireflies were not only rampant, but distractingly exotic. They not only blinked on and off, they did so in multiple colors, many looking like the eyes of unknown beasts. Sounds were also heard, a majority from insects, but there were also growls and screeches. The small, deep valley was a perfect acoustic amplifier. Sounds bounced off the valley walls like it was a concert hall. But the orchestra was invisible, and it likely had fangs and claws.

Chapter 10

BRIARS

We woke more tired than when we went to bed. How much energy is consumed during a restless night of sleep? Would it have been better just to stay up all night?

Before breaking camp the mercenaries polished their armor and weapons. Equivalent to making sure you wore clean underwear in case you got in an accident?

Scree Castle's escape tunnel terminated somewhere on the far end of Bramble Valley, at the base of the shear ridge the keep was built on. The dense foliage would likely require a meter by meter search.

An hour into our day's journey we passed through some briars with white flowers and dark berries. One of the mercenaries couldn't help himself. He had to sample the free food that was more aesthetically and psychologically pleasing than the trail rations he had been eating the past four days. Plucking the first berry was like pulling a trigger. The narrow fronds at the base of the vines swirled robustly as they rose. The trooper's flesh was torn apart and pulverized like it was put in a blender. The larger bits were mulched. They settled onto the soil, becoming a rich fertilizer.

The trooper's bones lay intact, polished white in his armor.

"May his re-creation not be mutated," spoke Sergeant Stub curtly as we detoured around the white-flowered berries. So little spoken, or effort made, in the eulogy. Was death becoming that commonplace?

"Aren't we going to at least save his possessions?" I asked. "In some form or another he'll return, won't he?"

"HOLD UP!" said Sergeant Stub. "I was so eager to complete the mission I bypassed prudence. I was going to pick it up on the way out, but if we do survive we probably won't be able to find this exact place again. One briar patch looks like another. Troopers Trout and Dust, cautiously return and retrieve Trooper Drum's armor, sword, and whatever else is salvageable. Don't touch the berries. If anything moves towards you abandon your mission. If Drum wants his armor bad enough he'll return to get it after he's re-created."

Troopers Trout and Dust proceeded slowly, simultaneously watching every direction. They shook out Trooper Drum's skeleton from his armor. His sword was the only other item found to be worthy of salvage. Once safely away from the white flowered berries we examined the pieces of metal. Small scratches covered them. How could vegetation slice into metal like that? Was there something magical about it? Water could cut too, in its solid form. Magic was just unexplained science.

The extra equipment was becoming a burden. Nine sets were carried by twelve men. I didn't include myself. When did the ratio of living men to dead become unrealistic? One to one? What then? Whose possessions would be left behind?

We reached the base of the cliffs about midday. Runoff from the mountains above had created a weeping wall, a wide trickle of water many stories tall. At the base of the water a bog had formed.

"Let's place all the extra gear here," said Sergeant Stub. He was referring to one of the few dry areas in the region, a squat rise about 20 meters from the weeping wall. "Time to start looking for that entrance. You six---that way. And the rest of you---this way.

41

Nimbus and I will stay here. Return immediately if you find a way in. We don't want to be in this swamp any longer than we have to be."

"How much better are our odds now that we've survived Below Zero Ridge and crossed Bramble Valley?" I asked Sergeant Stub.

"Every minute we survive our odds increase. We still have to find that tunnel, make our way to Scree Castle, and return alive."

"You're quite the pessimist."

"I consider myself a realist, but doesn't everyone. Optimism is realism to an optimist, as is pessimism to a pessimist. If I didn't believe in mankind's Negative nature I wouldn't have a job. Someone always wants to kill someone else. How could it be different on a penal colony? I now believe there is a possibility of succeeding. I didn't think so four days ago. I would give you three to one odds against at the moment."

"And that's optimistic?"

"For a pessimist." Sergeant Stub smiled.

"Won't dying mean losing all your equipment? If everyone dies there is no one to return it to you."

"Sometimes a bit of extra excitement or challenge is worth the possibility of losing it all."

"Now you're speaking like an optimist."

"Just a label."

A cacophony of rushed voices and movement penetrated the stale, murky air.

Sergeant Stub loaded a crossbow and handed it to me. "Hit that trigger when you want to release the bolt. Don't fire too eagerly. The closer your target the more likely you'll hit it." Sergeant Stub also loaded a crossbow for himself.

The extra height the rise added wasn't enough to see over the vegetation. Through the intermittent breaks in the trees and bushes I saw flashes of metallic glean. Four mercenaries stumbled onto the rise. "Crow and Rash were entangled by the vegetation," trooper Dust informed us. "Mounds of rotting leaves fell onto us from behind while we were searching the cliff side. We attempted to pull Crow out, but as we reached for him other mounds fell onto us. We all tripped at least once. Everyone but Rash was able to get back up. I don't think either one of them, Crow or Rash, could have survived. I nearly suffocated myself under the weight of that dense, wet foliage."

"These crossbows aren't going to be too effective against those MOUNDS," stated Sergeant Stub, setting his on the ground. "But everything has a weakness."

"How about fire?" I suggested.

"It might work, if the vegetation around here wasn't so wet. What else can destroy plants?"

"How about the other extreme? Cold. If we could bring them up to Below Zero Ridge, or the cold down here."

"Drought also kills plants," suggested Trooper Trout.

"We need to be more realistic. What can we implement NOW?"

Commotion was now heard coming from the other direction. This time only one trooper ran up the rise. Before he had time to explain his misfortunes, more than a dozen waist-tall bipedals blitzed us. Their skin was the color and texture of bark. Green fern-like leaves grew from the tops of their heads. Thorns were where fingers should have been. Their facial features were diminutive and darker, becoming almost invisible from a distance. In each arm they carried a spear as long as their body. They were thrown at us simultaneously. Surprisingly, my last thought was concern about insects being attracted to my bleeding wounds.

Chapter 11

RE-CREATION

I woke in that dream state where you could hear and partially sense what was going on, but you couldn't see anything. I was somewhere high. I could feel the sun and wind on me. I could feel gravity flow over me and drop, like I was on top of a waterfall. My body was sprawled, as sometimes I found it to be in the morning, every limb seeming to hang from a different side of the bed. I moved every movable part, in an attempt to take inventory of my physical state. Arms---yes. Legs---yes. Head---of course, yes. And....something wasn't right. I should have stopped there. Did I have more than two arms? That wasn't right, was it? I couldn't remember. And something else. Something behind me. It felt like that hole in your mouth after a tooth was removed, but in reverse. More like when a denture is added. But this didn't feel artificial. I tensed it, then wiggled. It hit me. It felt like a whip, but it wasn't as smooth. I repeated the process with my third and fourth arms. They felt trapped beneath me. I began to feel claustrophobic. I panicked. I opened my eyes.

Obsidian sat on the ground beside me, leaning against a boulder. He smiled. "You're finally awake."

"I don't feel so awake."

"In an hour or two your senses will return in full. Being re-created shocks one's system."

I looked down at myself. I didn't know how to respond.

"Yes, that's really you. You are one of those rare individuals thoroughly mutated during their first re-creation."

My body was 20 meters long now, scaly, its color varying

from yellow to red. Oh, and I now had wings and a tail. I tried to stand, but got about halfway before I fell back down.

"You'll regain your strength in time, some of it after the shock to your system wears off, the remainder after you eat, and eat, and eat. You'll need more than just a slice of bread or a drum stick. A sheep or a cow or a dozen turkeys should do."

"Is there a market for such a thing?"

"I don't think they'll sell to you even if there was. You'll have to provide for yourself."

"How do you know so much about this?"

Obsidian's form became blurry. It appeared almost gelatinous, then it grew. After it stabilized and re-solidified Obsidian was 10 meters longer than me.

"You're also a dragon."

"Drac we prefer to be called."

"Do...drak...have a hierarchy? Does size or longevity matter?"

"Not formally. We are much more solitary and independent than gents: humanoid giants. They tend to form gangs to support each other as they perform their mischief. Drak have no pack mentality. There are so few of us anyway that there would be only one pack. This world is large enough for us to have our own space."

"How many drak are there?"

"You are the thirteenth. It sounds ominous, doesn't it, and for some in our society, it is. Many of us believed that our population would peak at twelve, since that is the most we have ever had. After Sequoia left us we assumed ONE new drak would replace her. Your arrival and destined re-creation was...unexpected."

"Destined?"

"Every entity on Limbo has its unique energy signature, like fingerprints, or a retina image. Some of us call it the NAME OF THE SOUL. Draks, as a group, have a similar energy pattern, even before we are re-created into this form. Think of your first few years on Limbo as your embryo-hood. Your destiny was to become a drak."

"So you knew I was to be re-created into a drak when you

first met me?"

"That is why I met you. I am your mentor. We learned that an entity as powerful as a drak needs some guidance early in their existence. Not only might they hurt themselves, they may hurt others, carelessly."

"So drak are morally sound?

"Not all. Some of us never had mentors, and others were influenced by Negativity later in life. Drak now are at least given an opportunity."

"What now?"

"I train you in survival, and ascertain what abilities you have and assist in developing them."

"Will I be able to return to human form like you?"

"That depends on you. Most drak can't."

"Will I be able to breathe fire?"

"Fire is the most common discharge, but there is also frost and various debilitating gases."

"What can you do?"

Obsidian opened his mouth. I heard a crackle, then saw sparks in his mouth. A lightning bolt burst from it, striking a boulder 100 meters away, breaking it in two. "I also can expel a repulsion gas. I prefer that attack, because it doesn't do any permanent harm. The most negative of our kind aren't so charitable."

"You must belch first before expelling the repulsion gas, but how does the lightning work?"

"I don't really know. I just think about static energy building and it does. It's similar to creating saliva. Once the charge is large enough I spit it out."

I was able to sit up now, awkwardly. My rear legs were in proportion to my body, but my arms were small, not much larger than they were before I was mutated. I was too large to stand on my hind legs, and my arms were too weak to comfortably support my body while on all fours. It explains why dragons are always portrayed lying down---or flying.

When was I going to do that? That alone might compensate

for me no longer being human. I was surprisingly okay with what happened to me. Maybe if I was mutated into an ant or something I would be upset, but being a dragon did have its advantages. A lion might be king of the jungle, but a dragon was king of the world: patriarch of not only the forests, but the prairies and the mountains, and the air above it.

I was also okay with the concept of there being dragons on Limbo. Could they have been created from a random cluster of mutations? Unlikely, but a place like this---a penal colony---would be the perfect place for a creative---and nostalgic---geneticist to experiment.

I put most of my weight on my back legs and used my arms primarily for balance. I was in a more or less crouching position.

I concentrated on accumulating saliva. All I accumulated was saliva. I spit. The half-liter of saliva covered a small boulder. For some reason the excretory puddle was hilarious to me. I laughed in the manner I was capable. The dinosaur-like sound frightened me. The laughing irritated my throat, forcing me to cough. A burst of cold air erupted from my mouth.

"I think we discovered your breath weapon. And I believe you could use it both defensively and offensively, depending on the intensity and the duration. Now let's see if we can teach you to fly." Yes, let's do that.

It was about as difficult---or easy---as learning to ride a bike, with the consequences of a fall being more dire. Once I learned to glide, it became easier. Too much effort was required to keep my bulk moving. After a couple of hours I was able to take off and land fairly well, and keep myself aloft after I got up there. I wasn't able to maneuver very well, but Obsidian said that will gradually improve with practice, but I would never be that proficient at it, due to having to transfer so much weight.

I never became a shape-changer like Obsidian, but I was able to modify the weather, slightly. I didn't know how it worked, but whenever I wished for the wind to change directions, or the rain to fall, it did, with limited results. The control of winds helped me fly. I regretted not being able to return to Lizard Falls, but what I gained in my new form more than made up for it.

"Now it's time for you to find your own territory," said Obsidian.

"I thought I would stay here with you."

"You can visit if you like, every two or three years. Drak are loners. The Southern Spine is my territory."

"Where can I go? I've become accustomed to living on this mountain range."

"Then we need to find you another. The problem is most drak like mountains. The Raspberry Mountains are currently uninhabited. The range isn't as large as the Southern Spine, but the peaks are just as tall. The countryside surrounding them is beautiful and very isolated. If I hadn't been here so long I might let you have the Southern Spine, and immigrate to the Raspberry Mountains myself. We'll fly there tomorrow."

Chapter 12

RASPBERRY

Being larger and more experienced, Obsidian would persistently outdistance me. Whenever he noticed he would slow down enough for me to catch up with him, then fly off again.

There were four major seas in Limbo, interconnected by four straits that met at a smaller sea called the Crosshairs. We crossed the Western Strait. Obsidian mentioned how he wished he had settled down near water. Drak may be territorial, but they never lose their wanderlust. That, or someone else's home is always greener, wetter, cooler, more scenic....

The terrain we passed over varied, from the alpine rockiness of the Southern Spine, to the mixed conifer and deciduous forest of the Springwoods, to the dark swamps of Serpent Glade. After crossing the strait we passed over grassland, before it transitioned into pine at the foothills of the Raspberry Mountains. We saw few signs of civilization. There was a significant grouping of streets and buildings at Gulag, but the only other evidence of human habitation we saw at our cruising altitude was the Wizard's Tower. It was still under construction on the Southern Spine's tallest peak, 20 kays northeast of Gulag.

We landed in the center of the Raspberry Mountains, in a relatively flat, wide expanse. Wild flowers were abundant. The major peaks of the range rimmed the valley, performing the dual function of sentinels and fencing.

"There is one settlement in the foothills: Berry, to the southeast. It's a peaceful village. Its commerce consists of selling fruits and berries. If you keep to yourself the citizens of Berry shouldn't bother you. Cattle, sheep, deer, buffalo, antelope, and various fowl, including turkeys and pheasant, roam free in the prairie. I recommend not scavenging for food in the village."

"Do I just wander around like we've been doing since I became a drak?"

"Drak usually find a cave to live in, at least for sleeping."

"Do you have a cave?"

"Yes."

"And we didn't go there?"

"Drak prefer to retain their seclusion. And yes, we keep whatever treasure we have hidden, which can become substantial after accumulating it for decades. We are powerful enough not to die easily, and careful enough for it to not happen frequently."

"Aren't we then re-created like everyone else?"

"Yes, but not into a drak. We are limited to one draconian lifespan. After that we are re-created into something else."

"Is there anything more powerful than a drak?"

"In theory, but that type of existence isn't desired by the young."

49

An eerie, gravelly moaning was heard. It sounded like movement on a rocky road on a windy day. I noticed an oddly-shaped stone lying in the meadow near me. Had it always been there? It was five meters in diameter, and seemed to be a different shape every time I looked at it. I looked around. There were other boulders and stone fragments lying in the meadow, but none were as irregularly shaped. I heard the scraping sound again. It stopped when I turned toward the boulder.

"You weren't the first drak to reside here," Obsidian explained. "Amber Orchard Prairie lived here for 22 years. She was one of the first to be sentenced to Dartmoor. She lived in the Raspberry Mountains before humans settled here. It broke her heart when Berry was established. She became careless, and four years later was killed by a cryohydra."

"Are you telling me she was re-created into that rock?"

"In many ways elementals are a superior form of life. Events appear different to them. Being part of nature they sense things in ways we can't imagine. Time has slowed for them. We being here and speaking is like a mosquito flying in, buzzing for a bit, then hastily flying off."

"Elementals are connected to Limbo somehow?"

"They retain their sovereignty, but they are also linked to the world."

"Can we communicate with them?"

"Not really. Holistically they understand our intentions. Specifics happen too quickly for them to comprehend."

"Are drak the only mutants re-created into elementals?"

"The number of elementals would indicate otherwise. I must leave you now. It's been many days since I've been to my cave. Even when I was in Lizard Falls I periodically left to return home. You didn't think I wandered aimlessly in the prairie did you? I'll be back in a year to check up on you. A year after that is the 9th Draconic Gathering. Every four years the drak communicate with one another. It's much safer learning about the world that way than invading each other's territories. We also take a census. You'll be officially numbered among us then. A final bit of advice: don't enter another drak's territory unless absolutely necessary. A brief, friendly visit, or a quick passing through is allowed, but not always welcomed. An extended stay will prove deadly to one or both."

Obsidian pushed himself into the air with his massive hind legs, simultaneously flapping his wings. It took him just seconds to soar up to cruising altitude. He caught an aerial and glided towards the southeast.

"Well, Amber, it looks like it's just going to be you and me." I waddled over to the elemental. I must have moved too quickly for her, because the stone borrowed itself into the ground, disappearing.

All that flying made me hungry. I had hunted with Obsidian, but hadn't done well. He did most of the killing and shared what he caught: a rare occurrence indeed. Drak were legendarily greedy. If he hadn't been my mentor I would be a much thinner drak. The problem I had with hunting, other than never having to kill my own food before, was Obsidian watching me. I had become self-conscious. Now that I had a prairie full of food to myself I would do better. My first kill was a lame antelope. It was probably old to, but like playing pool, I took scrap. My hunting skills gradually improved, and I eventually caught animals that actually ran away from me. As time progressed my weekly hunting excursions became one of the few things I looked forward to.

The cryohydra that had killed Amber was beginning to get on my nerves. Every time I saw it in the distance I thought of Amber being killed by it. Its hissing wasn't very loud, but it was distinct enough that it gave me chills whenever I heard it. Simply seeing the silhouette of its shape made me angry. It had a breath weapon like my own, so our artilleries countered one another. It couldn't fly though and it didn't have teeth as sharp as mine, or talons. It didn't taste bad either. Winter had finally arrived, coating the meadow in white. The cold preserved its meat for an entire month. It was kind of bland, but nutritious.

A year later another cryohydra appeared. I killed that one too. Then another appeared. It was like playing a video game and

51

the creatures you just killed reappearing every couple of minutes. The terra-forming matrix that had created Limbo was designed by a computer. It was inevitable for there to be similarities. I considered allowing the next cryohydra re-creation to live, so another wouldn't take its place, but what guarantee was there that only one could exist in the same location. I returned to killing the cryohydras. With none of them living long enough to develop their skills they didn't put up much of a fight.

I tried to communicate with Amber, but wasn't very successful. Gradually we became comfortable with one another, actually hanging out after a dozen or so years. She sang to me when I was sad: eerie creaky, gravelly sounds full of emotion. She also began to sleep by my side in the cave I discovered at the base of one of those sentinel mountains. The cave was originally very cramped, but somehow it became more roomy. It had to be Amber's doing, because I wasn't shrinking. I was double my original length, and growing. My---informal---status among my kind grew. Some draks died. More were born. Our numbers slowly increased. There were now 23 of us. I must have been getting old, because I began complaining about the over-population of drak, and wishing for the good old days. Amber felt my concern and relayed to me that the draconian population would level off at two dozen.

Monotony may persist, but it wasn't perpetual. The risk of escaping it is it being a middle ground. Before the monotony could become unbearable my life changed---for the worse. I awoke like I normally did, my head resting against the brown nugget of granite---relative to my size---that was Amber. Some days she wouldn't leave the cave, and that would be okay with me. I felt more secure knowing she was safe there, and safely protecting my hoard of treasure. I was disciplined enough not to attack humans, but sometimes I still collected their personal items, including gold and gems. Humans died every day. I didn't have to kill them personally to take their treasure. I did occasionally kill those that killed them. Good deeds deserved to be well rewarded.

Chapter 13

GOLEM

I was compelled to leave the cave. I told myself it was my idea---my draconian senses providing awareness of a presence---but hunter or prey, it matters not, he who walks away wins in the end, in whatever form that takes.

I felt guilty whenever I left Amber alone. Did she feel abandoned? A lover jilted? A spouse left behind as her husband spent the day out with the boys? I wasn't even sure if Amber felt anything. There was an attachment between us, a familiarity, but was that due to mutual admiration or repetition?

The meadow was covered with wildflowers again. I loved their smell, especially after they first appeared, when the air was still cool from the last remnants of winter. If I knew that was going to be the last time I smelled them I would have relished them more.

A human was in the meadow, alone. The same extrinsic drive that compelled me to leave the cave drew me to him. Before I could reach him I found myself in another body. The transition wasn't instantaneous. There was a brief confusion, like that time as I child when I fell off a swing and hit my head. I was aware of my environment, but saw it through another's eyes. My torso, head, hands, and feet were made of stone. They were connected by sticks. My draconian body lay beside me. I almost fainted, the out of body experience being that powerful.

The human had to be a Wizard, a member of the most powerful elem---elemental energy---conglomerate on Limbo. There were rogue manipulators, but those powerful enough to perform a transfer of spirits likely mutated themselves out of humanity ages ago. Control was as important as raw power, and without years of accumulated study it was inevitably lost.

Transferring my essence from the magnificence of a drak to the jumble of rubble and deceased vegetation wasn't enough for the Wizard. He commanded me to pummel my former self. The compulsion was much greater than it had been to come to him. No longer in drak form, my draconian will had faded. I began walking to my former self. It was awkward at first performing the movements---the thing I had become wasn't built like a drak. Even more awkward, was being forced to destroy myself---what had been myself. The shell had been more than my physical representation. It encased my sense of self, my confidence. I became angry. I was no longer a drak in body, but I was still one in spirit. The enchantment was broken. Instead of pulverizing my former self I pulverized the Wizard, my stone hands acting like pestles, the earth beneath him the mortar.

Now that the Wizard was dead I would return to my drak body. It didn't happen. With much frustration I lunged toward the draconian carcass. Instead of the two bodies merging, I bounced back, toppling, but still intact.

I became depressed. I just stood there beside my former self for days. Amber eventually investigated what happened. I was too ashamed to face her, so I ran away. She initially attempted to follow me, but soon gave up, her speed being just a fraction of mine.

I moped around the meadow for weeks, weeks becoming months. My draconian carcass never decayed. At first it may have been residual elem---you didn't think something as exotic as a drak could exist without some assistance?---but eventually it froze when winter returned. The next cryohydra prospered, with me no longer being in a form capable of disposing of it. The climate also changed. The Raspberry Mountains had entered an ice age. With the combination of perpetual winter and the cryohydra run amuck, humans stopped passing through the mountains. It was safer and easier for them to go around.

Boredom began to set in. My artificial body no longer

needing food to sustain it, there was no need to hunt. It was fortunate. Being unable to fly, and the cryohydra consuming everything in the mountains, I probably would have starved to death. How did I subsist? Solar energy, perhaps, or a passive collection and processing of elem.

Chapter 14

COMPANIONS

My boredom was finally relieved when a mixed-race troop entered the meadow that was now an arctic plain. Since the passage through the mountains had been blocked by the cryohydra many groups have attempted its demise. All had failed. They actually added to the problem, adding protein to a diet that had become increasing vegetarian.

My misery had fed upon itself. Whatever residual draconian emotions I had had completely faded. I hated myself for allowing the condition I was in to exist. Hating and being hated for weeks upon weeks, months upon months, had taken its toll. I was no longer completely sane. To be aware of my insanity I knew I had not completely crossed over: a glance within, a foot testing the water, but not a full emersion. Emotions were a form of energy, and I was drained. Apathy set in. Being a creation of the elements, emotions may no longer be part of my composition. No, the emotions were still there, but distant, buried, hibernating, waiting for the warmth of spring that might never return to revive them. I considered destroying myself. Even if I didn't return as a drak, anything would be better than a mixed-media construct. But apathy won out. It took less energy---physically, mentally, and emotionally---to simply exist than to make such a drastic change in my condition.

I walked upon the polar plain aimlessly---it was more entertaining than standing in one place---until THEY interrupted the solitude of my bare existence. For the first time in months I felt a spark, a jolt, a pulse of emotion. Interaction, even non-verbal, added to my life. Maybe living was worthwhile. What was to come next? I was both frightened and excited for the question to be answered.

"I might as well come with you," I said to them. THEY were three humans and a gent.

"What if we don't want you to join us?" asked the largest of the humans---the unchanged, as the re-created called them.

"I think it's my decision where I go," I responded. "I guess you could try to run away from me, but I'll eventually catch up to you."

"Why would you even want to travel with us?" asked the tallest of the unchanged.

"I'm not too good about making decisions at the moment, so I thought you might make them for me." Allowing others to proxy as my inspiration may appear to be degrading, but it was less degrading than wandering aimlessly for an eternity.

"But you don't know where we're going," the third human commented. He didn't have as commanding of a prescience as the other two, but there was something within that was much greater. Whatever it was he had it. On Limbo they called it the GRACE OF GAEA: someone who was always in the right place at the right time. Charisma. Luck. Descriptors attached to intangibles. Characteristics and abilities that can't be explained or described.

On Limbo, Gaea was both legend and a deity. With nature taking such a prominent role it was reasonable, even predictable, such a figure would emerge. Originally EARTH MOTHER, Gaea has evolved into MOTHER EARTH. Gaea was not only the god who ruled the planet, she WAS the planet. Not only had the residual energies of the terraforming caused mutations and re-creations it had endowed the planet, its collective essence, with the spark of life. Many believe one's mutations aren't self-inflicted or random, but the decree of Gaea. The Frontiers didn't always exist. Extreme moral mutations weren't always segregated to the fringes of society.

"I imagine it won't be run of the mill, or you wouldn't be up here. I don't even mind if you all are crazy. I find crazy quite interesting. Never a boring day when you're crazy, no sir." I would know. But crazy did get boring after a while without stimulus.

"Don't you fear for your safety? With little effort we could pick you up and smash you against one of these boulders," stated the gent. As giants went he was relatively diminutive, just three meters tall from bald head to sandaled toe.

"Come along, if you wish," spoke the largest human, "if you think you're so bold, but do as we say or we will discard you the first opportunity that arises. Our quest will terminate when either a hydra is dead, or we are. Don't make any sounds or movements that will reveal our approach, or distract us once we're in battle."

After permitting my new companions to wander nearly as aimlessly as I had been when they found me I showed them where the cryohydra was. Incompetence was entertaining, but eventually becomes tedious. Implementing the advice I offered it still took them twice as long to defeat the creature as I ever took, on my worse day.

We returned to Berry City as heroes, WE meaning THEY. I was considered a mere toy, a toy forbidden to speak. Centaur, the largest human, explained it this way: "Golems are rare, but not unheard of. Self-willed golems, just rumors. Keep silent in public. The fewer questions that are asked, the better."

"I'll have to make up for my silence when we leave Berry City," I countered.

"I'm sure you will."

We had a playful banter even in the beginning, brothers that mocked as they punched each other in the shoulder and passed gas in their face. Centaur was not only the largest unchanged, but the eldest. From the looks of him he had to have been a bouncer before he was incarcerated. The tallest was named Stick. His comments about himself may have been considered boasting, if they weren't true. He was the finest swordsman in Limbo, and an Octagonal Knight. Protecting the moral balance was not an easy task on a planet where a majority of its inhabitants flaunted their Negative attributes. Then there was Hornet. He was of average build and attribute, but he had that GRACE OF GAEA thing going for him. The gent, well, was a gent. Pulp as he was called, was essentially a large human. Being re-created in Chapo---the Chaotically Positive Frontier---he mutated into a herbivore. His teeth and digestive track adapted, modifying his appearance, but not in an extreme manner.

In Berry City my companions were reunited with Hornet's mate: Dinga. She was an avian changeling, and pregnant. How could a sterile woman become pregnant? Many hypotheses: extreme randomness, freak mutations, the Will of Gaea. The latter was the most probable, for those who believed in Mother Earth: the Grace of Gaea had literally entered her. She lived with the local healer while her male traveling companions abandoned her to destroy the hydra. What a coup it was for him to have the first pregnant woman in the history of Limbo walk into his office.

Dinga squealed when she saw me. "YOU BROUGHT ME A GIFT!" I would have been more ecstatic at her bypassing the embrace of her husband to be in my prescience if she didn't give me that attention because she thought I was a toy.

Not knowing how to react I just stood there. With the healer present it was my duty to remain silent. I was not the type of person to retain my unease. I would have rather walked 50 kays or jumped off a cliff than keep my mouth shut.

It was decided the healer would be included in our inner circle, not just about my true existence, but something significantly more important that I hadn't yet been made aware of. The healer was no friend to the Wizards. He bypassed the retail elemental energy market, creating his own elem through the combining of certain herbs. Elem itself didn't have any mystical powers, but when combined with others of its kind---five total---there was a significant release of elemental energy. These penta, as they were called, could strike a person with lightening, or bring them back from near-death. Science or magic? Explained or unexplained? Different names for the achievement of the same goal. The healer's agenda was simple: to heal, with the most efficient means possible. If he could do so for a tenth of the price the Wizards charged....

Chapter 15

PORTAL

Hornet removed a green sphere from his backpack. Centaur, a blue sphere from his. They were brought together. When they were about a meter apart Centaur released his. The forces of attraction and repulsion were so perfectly balanced, the blue sphere floated freely.

"Do you think the next sphere could have moved that much since the last time we checked it?" Hornet questioned.

"Unlikely," said Centaur.

"But we have," said Dinga.

"But not enough to change the angle that much. Unless...."

"What?" asked Hornet.

"Unless there's another sphere"

"Aren't there four more spheres?" asked Dinga.

"Are you saying the spheres are now reacting to a different piece of the portal?" Stick concluded. "Than the one they reacted to in Gnotting Hill?"

That's why the spheres looked familiar. They formed a portal---a portable one. The information was fascinating, but not life altering. I didn't intend to leave Limbo. In this form was it even possible? If I became a drak again, what kind of life would I have off-world?

"So, we're now closer to the fourth sphere than the third?" Dinga conjectured.

"We're much closer," said Hornet. "The pressure is at least twice as much as it was in the Copper Forest."

"So we're almost there. The next sphere isn't in the Negative Frontier." Relief flooded Pulp's features. Those residing in the moral extremes were distressed by their counterparts in the opposing extremes.

Centaur unrolled his map. We were in the center of the western peninsula, formed by the convergence of the Northern and Western Straits at the Crosshairs. "How strong a pull do you estimate it to be, relative to what it was in the Copper Forest? More than twice?"

"Almost three times," Hornet answered.

Centaur placed his finger on the far coast of the Northern Strait.

"So it might be on an island," said Pulp.

"Or underwater," Stick added. Dinga squirmed.

The error was obvious. "The force of attraction between two bodies is inversely proportional to the square of the distance between them," I reminded them. Blank stares. "It means the forces between them increase at a greater rate than the distance between them."

Dinga frowned. "So we're not as close as we thought?"

Centaur recalculated, placing his finger on a new location. "Beyond the Northern Spine, but still in Neutrality?"

Pulp moved Centaur's finger further east. "I guess I had to return to the Negative Frontier eventually."

"I didn't think Positives ventured that far from home," Hornet commented.

"Let's just say I didn't always live in the Copper Forest. Let's leave it at that."

"How many weeks do you think it will take?"

"Three weeks," Stick conjectured.

"We've come almost halfway and it's only taken us two weeks," Centaur scrutinized.

"As the crow flies. There's a significant body of water between us and the Northern Spine. Then there's the crossing of the mountains."

Hornet looked at Dinga hesitantly. "How much of that younger version of yourself is still in you? Can she convince you to take one more sea voyage?" He traced the route a ship might make with a finger. "We could completely bypass the Northern Spine if we traveled by boat."

"NO BOAT!" Dinga barked. Her emotions got the best of her. She broke down, concealing her sobs in Hornet's shoulder.

"So a dry journey it is," stated Centaur matter-of-factly.

Yes, instead of crossing the sea and saving three weeks we had to walk around the water, because someone was afraid of getting wet. I liked Dinga---she was by far my favorite, of those I traveled with---but she was a girl, and at times acted like it.

It was an arduous journey. If it wasn't for the high probability of meeting Wizards---and enacting my revenge upon them---I would have abandoned my associates.

The Healer considered joining us, but determined he could be of better use where he was, healing the Berrillians as he continued his studies in herbology.

We did add another member to our group, in the Platinum Mountains. A trog general named Paint joined us to prove to his people that they weren't under the influence of moral manipulation. It was hypothesized that pockets of Negativity existed beneath the ground, popping up in seemingly random locations, like veins of precious ore. One of the pockets was apparently ruptured as the trogs expanded their city. Theory transitioned to fact when General Paint began to notice the ethical changes within him. The longer he was away from Trogdom, diminishing the effects, the more aware he became.

Although tedious, the journey wasn't unbearable---until I

met others of my kind---what used to be my kind. The embarrassment was devastating. Can you imagine, transforming from a drak to an artificial construct---A GOLEM!?

We found the third sphere, but not without difficulty. After fighting through an army of gobs, and nearly as many hobs, we were confronted by a floating orb. The guardian of the Amethyst Pearl was a disciple of Lord Hide, a gent living in Orneg---the Ordered Negative Frontier. The Brotherhood of Giants prevented one gent from harming another, but that didn't prevent their minions from attacking---or being attacked---inadvertently.

The guardian appeared, initially, to be a helium-filled balloon. As it floated above us a gigantic eye was released from its body, the elongated appendage it was attached to making it look like a turtle coming out of its shell. The iris was multi-faceted, resembling a bloodshot sunflower. Tendrils stuck out from the orb, wiggling like worms. At the end of each was an eye: miniature versions of their host.

My companions became mesmerized. No longer consisting of flesh and blood, I was immune.

Centaur was first to be attacked. One of the tendril-eyes winked at him. He turned to stone.

Another stared at Stick. He was set aflame. As he fell to ground, his flesh turned to charcoal, a burst of energy fled from his body. Someone not attuned to the elements wouldn't have spotted it. It was transparent, but with the slightest of contours, resembling a heat wave. His armor was smudged by the seared carbon, but it appeared to be undamaged. Spontaneously, it evaporated, like water on a hot surface. His charcoaled remains crumbled. I would have continued to stare in the direction of these odd events if the remainder of my companions weren't engaged in the fight of their lives.

I was struck by lightning, but instead of shattering my wood and stone body, it dissipated. I had absorbed the energy.

General Paint had gone insane. He randomly struck out, hitting his companions as often as his adversary.

Hornet knocked him unconscious from behind, but not before the trog struck Centaur's stone body, breaking off one of his fingers.

Hornet was spared, none of the orb's attacks against him able to make contact. It would have been a miracle if it didn't happen so consistently. The Grace of Gaea had saved him, again.

Pulp was struck by a glancing burst of frigid air. His left arm was blackened from the frost bite. The attack breaking his trance, he charged the orb.

Dinga hadn't been assailed yet, her less aggressive nature---she didn't want to harm her unborn child---distancing her from the battle.

Hornet, being protective of his wife, wasn't an effective offensive threat. That left me. I never intended to be an active participant, in this altercation or any other, but if I wished our journey to continue, so I might have that opportunity to enact my revenge, a semblance of our party had to remain intact. To be completely honest, that wasn't the only reason I choose to assist my companions. I was becoming attached to them----more like an owner of a pet than as a friend---but there was still that fellowship there that I would miss if they all died and were re-created many kays from me.

I charged the orb, absorbing the brunt of it attacks. I hit it with as much force as my small body could generate. My stone hands ruptured the orb membrane, splattering me with yellow goo. I climbed to the top of the granite prism. After plucking the purple metallic sphere from the tapered pedestal cresting it, I jumped down. I wasn't concerned I might have been harmed, after all I was just made of sticks-and-stones.

Chapter 16

LINT

We dragged ourselves back to Quantum, a hamlet on one of the western hills of the Twin Hills. The hills were actually a cluster, being named for the two tallest peaks. Being small, Quantum didn't have any penta to sell, not even healing stones. As I spent decades in solitude, the Wizards honed their distribution skills. They bundled penta into easy-to-use forms: single-use capsules (more commonly referred to as stones), multi-use rods, and perpetual-use rings. The rings were their greatest achievement. Through decades of research they discovered that if a certain number of elem could be clustered in a contained space they would become self-propagating. There were two theories. The first: that elem were spawned, by cloning or fission. The second: a magnetic field was created, drawing free elem into the collective.

We returned to the cottage we rented prior to obtaining the purple sphere. Ongoing, swirling, heated discussions, on our next course of action, persisted into the night.

"We need to find a healer," spoke Dinga in a manner all women did when they intended their words to be more than suggestion.

"I'll be okay," said Centaur. "The finger is on my offhand."

"But can Pulp get by with a dead arm? If we don't heal it soon, we'll have to amputate to save the rest of him."

"It doesn't hurt," the gent responded.

"That's because it's dead. MEN! They never want to go to the doctor. And how about General Paint? He's no longer trying to attack anything that moves...because he's catatonic."

"We did recover the sphere," I added. That brightened the mood, momentarily.

"Let's see what happens when it comes into contact with the other two." Hornet removed the green sphere from his pack. Centaur did the same with the blue.

Dinga held the purple. As she moved it closer to the other two she abruptly stopped. "Someone else better take this. I don't want to risk harming the baby."

Pulp snatched it with his healthy hand.

Centaur brought his sphere closer to Hornet's. When they were about a meter apart he released it. The attractive, repulsive, and gravitational forces strained Hornet---noticeable, but not debilitating. When Pulp brought his sphere closer, Hornet struggled to not spin around. Slowly, he rotated, stopping when the purple sphere was about a meter from the blue. "The attraction to the blue is nearly as strong as the repulsion to the green," he said.

"Should I release my sphere?" asked Pulp. Hornet nodded. He was nearly knocked to the ground as the purple sphere fell to the ground, dragging the blue and green spheres behind it.

"It might be better if you held the middle sphere," I suggested.

Hornet set the green sphere on the ground, then moved to the blue, which he picked up with both hands. The green and purple spheres remained on the ground. Using an overhand grip he rotated the green sphere. The other two spheres slowly lifted off the ground. With his back bent backwards and his biceps straining, the semi-circular plane the three spheres formed eventually became parallel to the ground. "One more sphere and you'll have to lift these, Centaur."

"Or we could just set them on the ground," I commented.

"Didn't you just suggest I should hold them?"

"It's disappointing for me too. Watching you juggle wasn't as pleasurable as I thought it would be. I'm still uncertain whether I lack emotions, or they're just severely dampened."

Hornet would have dropped the spheres if there wasn't the possibility of them breaking. He sent them down abruptly instead.

"Anyone want to take bets on how far I can kick the thing?" asked Centaur.

Pulp was shocked.

"He did just save us," Hornet commented after he stretched out his back. "And you'll probably break off a toe trying it."

"I'm willing to test the hypothesis," I volunteered. It was definitely more fun following these guys around than staying in that frozen meadow. It was unlikely I would be damaged in a tumble. Even if my dowels became detached they could be reset in the stone sockets.

Dinga put her hands on her hips. "Do I need to give you all a timeout?"

If I was capable, I would have laughed. My companions did--- except for Dinga. She had been serious. Ultimately, the cackling became too contagious. The moment became more important than the events leading up to it. She was crying before the emotions had run their course. The accumulative stress had to be released. There were worse ways.

As my companions took a moment to silently compose themselves, I examined the partially constructed portal. "It looks like the next sphere is south-southeast of here." I lifted the middle sphere. "I don't have a reference to compare it to, but there doesn't appear to be much force exerted in that direction."

Dinga's expression soured. "Which means it's quite a ways away."

Hornet lifted the sphere to confirm. "The pull is weaker than it was in Orpo."

"GREAT!" grumbled Centaur. "Why couldn't it be just a few kays away, like it was between the green and blue spheres?"

"There is the possibility that the more spheres attached the stronger the attraction to one another, causing the attraction to distant spheres to lessen," I said.

Hornet and Dinga discussed something in a corner of the cottage. The volume and emotional intensity escalated.

"I WILL NOT!"

"Think of the baby. You said you would return to Berry City."

"But that was to be late in my pregnancy."

I had to intervene. When you were as old as I was you didn't care what anyone thought of you. "If not for the well-being of yourself, or the baby, think of the welfare of others in our group. You hid at the edge of the battle, and YOU stood in front of her, trying to protect her, forgetting about the rest of us." Before they could respond with a rude rejoinder or an emotional meltdown, I added, "THINK about what I said." Living decades I became more in tune with the passage of time. I was not easily riled. I understood what bothered me now would be insignificant years later. Youngsters---those living less than an off-world life expectancy--- always lashed out when they felt upset. It was a reflex mechanism to immediately solve a problem that to them would continue until the end of time. There was only NOW and what stood directly in front of them. The future didn't exist.

After a good night's sleep---the passage of time did wonders putting things in perspective---the group finally agreed to travel to a larger settlement, one that had a healer, but....

"Northern Roost is closest," stated Dinga.

"But in the wrong direction," Centaur countered. "Blowing Sand is just a day farther."

"A day more might be a day too long. We're going to have to amputate Pulp's arm soon."

"I can make it another day," Pulp insisted.

"And Norport is just two days south of there, where Dinga can buy passage on a ship that will return her to Berry City," said Hornet.

"I'm not traveling by ship when I chose to return," Dinga insisted.

Before we left Quantum Dinga made a purchase. "It's an elem collector," she explained. "You remember Claw and Thrumbringer? They were elem prospectors. Combining what I learned from them and the Healer...."

"You're going to create a healing elixir," Centaur

hypothesized.

"If I collect the right elem and mix then in the proper manner."

"Before I mutated into a gent I dabbled in herbology," said Pulp. "Elem concentrates in certain vegetation, as it does in some mutants."

"Any assistance would be appreciated, and you'll be the immediate beneficiary of it."

As we packed, Dinga fished for elem. Not having any possessions I was free to observe her. The more I learned about elem, in whatever form it might take, the greater the possibility of recovering my greatness. "You see that sparkle," she said to me. "That's elem aero. There isn't much of it in this low of altitude. It's more numerous in the mountains." Was that why drak were so powerful?

Dinga swung the metal rod out before her, attempting to capture the glittery speck. Whenever she was almost upon it, it would rush away, like it was an annoying insect you wanted to slap. "I'm my own worst enemy," she enlightened. "The breeze I create with the rod's movement pushes the elem away. I need to be downwind." She maneuvered around the speck. She apparently found the spot she wanted because she began thrusting the rod again. "Now if I can get within 20 sims of it, hitting this trigger should capture it like lint in a vacuum. AH! There's one." Dinga twisted the rod. A small amber dot was revealed. "I need at least one more. FEEK! How am I going to store another variety? There are separate compartments to prevent the elem from mixing, but releasing them will be messy. No. Even if I was willing to risk it, isn't there a safeguard built in to prevent that from happening? For more than one variety of elem to be collected in the same collection rod? Can you return to the pub and buy three more collectors if it has them?" In hamlets and small villages pubs provided more than alcohol. They were restaurants and general good stores. Sometimes, even city halls.

"I don't think they'll sell to my kind, but I'll mention it to one of the others."

Centaur successfully bought the pub's remaining three elem collectors. In a peaceful community of this size supplies were limited, but in the Negative Frontier inhabitants were less risk sensitive. Goods that had the potential to generate a quick buck were readily available.

Chapter 17

RUMBLING

General Paint could walk, but not much else. Traveling on flat ground in a straight line was easy enough for him, but hiking down a hill via switchbacks was going to create some difficulty. His wits not yet recovered, General Paint didn't have the mental faculty to change course. Not only was his decision making impaired--- non-existent, actually---he wasn't even aware of his existence. He was in a vegetative state, but one where the vegetables could walk. Simple commands he was able to follow. Maybe his extensive military training kicked in, reacting without thinking. Stick and Centaur walked beside him, one on each side, to prevent the slightest deviation of movement tossing him off a cliff.

Pulp's arm was looking worse. It was beginning to smell, and the rot was expanding, almost to his shoulder. We traveled south to Blowing Sand. I feared we may have made a bad decision. Yes, I actually cared about someone other than myself. An affinity had developed between myself and my companions, even for the gent. Draks and gents have a relationship similar to cats and dogs. Historically, antagonists, but given the opportunity to cohabitate they often became the best of friends.

The road to Blowing Sand first wound its way around some of the smaller knolls of the Twin Hills, then followed the banks of Grit Creek. The water was as sediment filled as its name suggested. The Twin Hills, not too long ago, must have been mountains, before the creek began to shrink them. At Blowing Sand the creek merged with the Serpent River, which eventually flowed into the Eastern Sea at Newport. The washing away of the Twin Hills was what supposedly created the Rainbow Isles.

As we stopped for lunch Dinga fished for elem in the creek. "It would be easier if the creek was clear," she told me. "Clarity doesn't increase their number, but it does make them easier to see. The sea is where we should be if we we're serious about collecting elem aqua, farther from land the better. Help me look. The sparkles are blue." Dinga extended the rod to its full two meter length. "When the rod has some elem in it, it acts as a mild attractant, like bait. What I'm doing with an empty rod is equivalent to fishing with a cane pole."

"THERE'S ONE OVER THERE!" I shrieked. When was the last time I had been this excited? Not since becoming a golem. Elem collecting was like gambling, but without the possibility of losing. Through much patience Dinga captured the glowing blue spec. The next couple we spotted she wasn't as successful with, losing them before she was able to snare them. Dinga persisted in fishing for elem until she had captured three of them. She needed one more. The other members of our group became impatient with us when our prospecting carried us past the time we allotted for the lunch break.

"But it takes four elem aqua for one healing elixir," Dinga insisted.

"We'll be following the creek for two days," Hornet countered.

Dinga sighed. "All right."

"What type of elem must be added to elem aqua to create a healing penta?" I asked. I was not the type of person who accepted on faith. I needed to know how things worked.

"It depends on the type of healing. For Pulp's arm to heal properly he needs both a Disease Healing and a Flesh Healing penta. If what consumes his arm isn't destroyed it will return to eating it after it's made whole. There's also an Energy Healing penta. Pulp's stamina is strong enough without it. I haven't heard of any mutations caused by consuming unnecessary penta, but why risk it? Disease healing requires elem fiero. It will be easy to find in the desert surrounding Blowing Sand. Now elem terra, required for flesh healing, that will give us the most trouble. They are usually found in areas of dense vegetation, primarily forests."

"Deserts have oases don't they?" suggested Centaur. Being our leader he felt responsible for our well-being. It wasn't token sentiment. When someone was hurting he was hurting. The sympathy pains might have been psychological, but that didn't mean they were any less uncomfortable.

The terrain began to get dryer. Less vegetation was beside the road, and what was there looked brittle, and was coated in dust. The dimness that had been our constant companion since entering the Negative Frontier was still present, but it began to lessen. A light had been turned on, but behind a curtain. The sage and sparse grasses were as washed out as the sky. It began to get warmer, first just noticeably so, then unpleasantly.

"Do pregnant women always feel miserable in the heat?" asked Dinga.

"Second thoughts on wanting to be part of this adventure?" asked Hornet smugly.

"Second thoughts on wanting female companionship before I head back to Berry City?"

"Is there any elem fiero around here?" asked Centaur.

"Unlikely, but there is a POSSIBILITY of it now. The closer we get to the heart of the desert the more concentrated it will be. The sparkly specks will be red. If we can find sand dunes we're almost guaranteed to find some."

As my companions scanned the ground the best they could while walking, I began to sense a presence. It was a weak sensation, but growing steadily in intensity. We were heading towards it. "HOLD UP!"

It felt draconian, but it wasn't coming towards us from the sky, or the ground---but beneath it. That's why it felt so odd. It was borrowing through the earth, like a worm.

"Did you find elem fiero?" asked Dinga.

"A visitor," I replied. "It will be here in a minute, maybe less. Attack its underside, where it's most vulnerable. Its tail can pulverize, but if you face it directly you'll certainly die, being burned, frozen...."

"IT'S A DRAGON!?" Hornet barked.

"I don't think I've ever heard of a borrowing drak," Pulp commented.

"Neither have I," I said, "but I've been out of the loop for a while---but not that long. This drak can't be that old. It will be inexperienced. And relatively small---barely 20 meters long. Whatever it discharges won't have a range much farther than that."

We heard a rumbling beneath the ground, like an earthquake beginning, or a volcano or geyser about to erupt. Almost directly below us earth rose, forming a small hill. The upraised earth exploded, sending sand and dust in every direction. I was the only one in our party not temporarily blinded by the fine debris. I hastily studied the creature, attempting to ascertain its strengths and weaknesses. Its arms and legs were nearly non-existent, more likely genetic remnants of its prototypes than functioning appendages. It didn't have wings at all, which meant it couldn't fly. Its borrowing ability compensated for it, particularly in defense and surprising its prey. Its facial features were blunted. The most shocking were its eyes. They were white. THAT'S IT! "It's blind, or nearly so. It doesn't SEE with its eyes. It reacts to sound, or vibrations. The less you move the less likely it will become aware of you. Try to not make any sounds."

My companions stopped in their tracks. It must have confused the sand drak, because it stopped moving, just meters from Hornet, who stood protectively in front of Dinga. How finely tuned were the drak's senses? Could it hear breathing or even heart beats? Perhaps when it became older, when it had time to develop its senses. Something moved about 50 meters away. The drak moved slowly towards the sound, about half the speed a human walks. A jackrabbit hearing the predator, hopped away. The sand drak followed over land first, its coils rolling forward like a tank's treads. Aware it was losing ground, it borrowed back into the earth. "Stay still for another minute or two," I whispered.

The sand drak continued to move away from us. "You may move now, but keep your movements minimal and don't talk loudly."

"Did your luck save all of us this time?" Dinga asked Hornet.

"You wouldn't be alive if the drak was mature," I declared. "A juvenile drak has the might, but not the wit yet to dominate an encounter like this?"

"Is that elem fiero?" asked Hornet. He was referring to the glowing red speck on top of the mound the sand drak created.

It took less than a minute for Dinga to retrieve a collecting rod from her pack and suck up the particle, confirming its identity. "We'll see in a couple of minutes if I'm an alchemist. We need some type of binding agent: a few mils of water?"

Centaur filled the lid of his water flask. He handed it to Dinga. "This isn't going to destroy the lid? I prefer to not cross a desert with most of my water sloshing out." Perspiration beading on his forehead fell at that instant for emphasis.

"I hope not. If something goes wrong more than this lid will be damaged." Dinga discharged, first, four elem aqua into the water, then a single elem fiero. She swirled the liquid carefully. The sparkles collided. Their luminescence vanished after a brief escalation in intensity. The liquid was now a pale lavender. "If the injury was small enough to be completely immersed in the liquid I would apply the elixir directly to it. Since your entire arm can't be, I think it best you drink it, Pulp. Results won't be instantaneously, but the healing will eventually reach where it needs to."

Pulp cautiously drank the liquid in one swallow. "I'm still alive."

We watched him as he stood silently and motionless. He

breathed steadily and deeply. His damaged arm began to change color. The red, yellows, and greens began to fade. The black remained. The texture became smoother.

The gent sighed. "You don't notice how bad you feel until you start feeling better. You don't realize that feeling that way isn't normal."

"Can you feel your arm yet?" asked Centaur.

Pulp shook his head.

"Before he can be completely healed we need to find elem terra," said Dinga. "The deadness won't affect the remainder of his body, but he'll lose his arm soon if it isn't healed. The disease healing bought it another couple of days."

One member of our party partially healed, one to go. The trog had been in his near vegetable state for so long it was difficult thinking of him as more than just something you lugged around, like luggage. "We need to heal General Paint, too," I insisted.

"We need to find another elem fiero, then," said Dinga. "And some more elem aqua."

"Let's head a little farther south before setting up camp," Centaur suggested, "in case the drak returns. An hour more of hiking will still leave us with enough time to hunt for elem before it gets dark."

We hiked another 10 kilometers before stopping. It was amazing what a bit of danger does to one's velocity.

Dinga fished for elem aqua along Grit Creek while the rest of us searched for the more elusive elem fiero. Being more in tune with elemental energy than the others, I found it. It glowed exceptionally bright in contrast to the sundim.

"We should wait until morning to administer the elixir to General Paint," said Dinga. "He'll be confused when he comes out of his coma. It'll be better if he does so in daylight."

"So where is this oasis you spoke of?" Hornet asked Centaur. The desert became more barren with every kay.

"Blowing Sand will have some vegetation," Centaur retorted.

"But too many people," I added. "What are the odds, you think, of us finding an elem instead of one of its 700 inhabitants? Elem has a tendency to reconstitute itself, often in the same place, like re-creation nodes."

"I wasn't aware that happened," stated Dinga, "with elem or re-creations."

"What did you think then was the reason for there being so many large clusters of mutants?"

"People with similar personalities and hobbies...."

"...will congregate, but not easily on Limbo. Communication and transportation is rudimentary."

"Is it possible to stake a claim to one of these nodes?" Hornet asked.

"Some probably have, at least informally," said Centaur. "If I was aware of a node I would keep it secret. It would be easier than having to guard it. There are too many greedy people on Limbo, and life isn't dear enough with re-creation as insurance."

"There's a jungle near the coast," I suggested.

"Will we reach it in time?" Dinga asked

"We might, if we hasten our pace and limit our breaks," Centaur answered.

"There might be another possibility," said Pulp. "There is an oasis to the west of here."

"And you mention this NOW? It's you we're trying to heal."

"Lord Coal, one of my less benevolent brothers, controls it."

"You don't think he would grant you permission to search for a single elem?" asked Dinga.

"It's not that simple, negotiating with a gent from the Negative Frontier. You remember Lord Hide?"

"But wasn't that because we wanted to take the Amethyst Pearl from him?" asked Centaur. "There are thousands of elem."

"I will ask him," Pulp responded without passion, "but it won't be without cost."

"We have some gold," said Centaur.

"Gold isn't what he seeks." Pulp didn't elaborate.

Requiring no sleep I was the night watch, again. My

companions complained it was difficult to fall asleep with the heat. It didn't bother me---as long as it wasn't hot enough to burn wood.

Chapter 18

AHH, HEE, HAH

I thought about elem and its relationship to matter as my companions slept. Could everything on Limbo be explained as clusters of penta? Could penta runes replace organic chemistry diagrams? How does a golem differ from a drak?

My thoughts were interrupted by Dinga rising early and vomiting at the edge of camp. After washing her face in the creek, she sat next to me. "Isn't it amazing?" Exactly what I was thinking: it took skill to discharge a partially-digested meal like that. "I never thought I would be a mother, not with the lifestyle I lived." Dinga had been a prostitute, an upper-end prostitute, but still a prostitute. It may have been legal what she did, but so was gambling and auto racing. "If I knew I would have children one day I may have lived my life differently. How strange is it that now, living in this precarious place where no one can have children, I become pregnant? I should be the last person given the opportunity. Am I a double negative? Does doing two wrongs make it right? Having a child here and now seems wrong, but it feels right. You wouldn't have any peanut butter on you? Sorry. You don't have pockets."

"Or eat."

"Then how do you....?"

"That's still to be determined."

"Do you miss not being able to eat? I think I would."

"If frees up a lot of time."

"To do what?"

What indeed. "It eliminates urination and defecation. I miss peeing, outdoors."

"You wouldn't if you were a woman."

"Accuracy and distance---and creativity---are tested."

"Everything is a game to men, isn't it? I should return to Berry, shouldn't I? It's best for everyone, but me. I don't want to miss out on anything."

"In a couple of months you'll be experiencing something none of us ever will."

Dinga was silent for a moment. "I could study elixir creation while I was there. And perhaps establish an order to counter the Wizards in their high tower in Gulag. What would be the opposite of what they do?"

"Doing something down to earth, away from civilization."

"DRUIDS! I could establish a society of druids. The Limboan Druid Society: LDS. It would have to be in Berry. Near, not in.

"I'm too worked up to go back to sleep. I'm going to fish for more elem aqua. We'll be leaving the creek tomorrow. It might be awhile before we're this close to so much water."

General Paint was given the Disease Healing elixir after everyone woke. It took five minutes before he exhibited clarity. About ten before he could talk. "I apologize for falling asleep," he said. "I accept, without argument or discussion, your reprimand. Such an egregious dereliction of duty mustn't go unpunished.... It appears we're no longer in the Quad Depression.... Time for breakfast? I'm starving."

"Does he need another dose?" asked Hornet.

"He appears normal to me, but I've spent the past two decades in the Chaotic Frontier," said Pulp.

"Disorientation is expected," I said. "It took a while before I gathered my senses after I was transformed."

"So you were like this before you became a golem?" Dinga

asked.

That was the disadvantage of spending so much time with someone: they got to know you almost as much as you got to know them. "Let's just say those characteristics that I did retain didn't return immediately, not all of them. It took days for my bewilderment to abate."

"Days?"

"Being as ordered as General Paint is, his recovery will be expedited."

"It feels like it did after drinking too many beers---before I became a trog," General Paint shared. "You don't think I'm also going to have a hangover? I enjoyed the tingling and the camaraderie, and the fights, but not the nausea and headaches."

"You miss the chaos?" Pulp asserted.

"Hardly. Circumventing discomfort compensates for not experiencing joy."

"How can it?" asked Dinga. "Without joy is life worth living? The climb up a hill is compensation for the view."

How about someone like me who doesn't embrace order or chaos? Does that make me a eunuch?

"We're two days south of the Twin Hills," Centaur informed the trog.

"I've been asleep that long?"

"Not exactly asleep. Your mind perhaps, but not your body."

"I was a...zombie?" General Paint's breathing intensified. His eyes became large. They scanned, looking for an opening if he needed to flee. It was disconcerting to see someone so powerful and orderly so terrified.

"Your body isn't decaying," Dinga assured him. "You haven't been possessed."

"That orb that attacked us did this to you," Centaur explained. "It made you delusional. Dinga crafted an elixir that healed you."

"Thank you, Lady Dinga. I've been under immoral influence

78

for years, and days after the effects have finally worn off I lose my mind. It will be welcomed to return to normalcy, whatever that may be. Did I miss anything?"

"We escaped a sand drak," said Centaur.

"And I missed it." The trog became depressed.

"But we're going to meet a malevolent gent later today."

General Paint perked up. "You're not just saying that?"

"We don't intend to attack him," Hornet added. The trog's smile dissolved briefly, but returned. I don't think he believed Lord Coal would be that peaceful.

The farther we traveled from the creek the drier it got, initially cracked earth, transitioning into sand.

"Is that the oasis?" asked Hornet. "I think I see water."

"It's a mirage," I said. "Sand elementals are notorious tricksters. You can tell if the image is real if you know what you're looking for. The desert is flat here, so the horizon should be at our level or slightly below, due to the curvature of the planet. The pool of water is slightly above the horizon."

"Why do sand elementals go to the effort?" asked Dinga.

"Like most mutants it probably comes naturally to them. The mirages are a defense mechanism. Where do travelers, human, animal, or mutant wish to travel to in the desert? To water. So the sand elementals project the image of water in a direction away from them, so they won't be bothered."

We entered salt flats an hour later. "How much farther?" asked Dinga.

"I don't know...exactly," Pulp responded. "I've never traveled to Pyramid Sands by foot."

"HEE, HAH!" exclaimed a deep piercing voice, wickedly. "What could be more pathetic? Going willfully to the pyramid or not being able to find it?"

Liquid bronze pooled in front of us. Once a considerable volume of it had oozed out from the salt flats, it rose and began to take shape. It became roughly human, but twice as tall. It stood immobile a moment, looking like a metal statue. Had it always been there, and we had imagined the rest? It moved again, rending

79

our reality. It strolled two steps closer to us, then stopped.

"I could kill you all, except for the one that Gaea protects. But for what purpose? You may react a bit before you die, entertaining me, then what? None of you would be re-created nearby, so I wouldn't be able to torment you again, at least not soon."

"What is this arrogant thing?" asked Centaur.

"It's a djinn," I answered. "They have been given extraordinary powers by Gaea, but at an equally extraordinary price."

"And that price isn't to be paid to you, past glory," spoke the djinn to me. "Even I couldn't return you to the body you were unworthy to keep."

"What do you wish with us?" asked Dinga. "We have urgent matters to attend."

"What I'm doing now: conversing, relishing your reactions. Perhaps I will detain you just long enough for the gent to lose that arm. It might be hilarious to watch it fall off. Or maybe I'll detain you longer, to witness you giving birth. I've heard it's the most excruciating of experiences."

"What makes you think we can't defeat you?" asked General Paint.

"Because, if on the unlikely possibility I am destroyed, I will be re-created almost instantaneously---another of Gaea's gifts to my kind. My power is great. The complexity of my body isn't. It is 100 percent bronze. How many times will you have to defeat me before you can escape the salt flats?"

"So you can't leave the salt flats?" Everyone---and thing---has weaknesses. The difficulty is in finding them, in time to be of use to you.

"Immaterial. You are in my domain."

"There must be something we can do for you," spoke Centaur, "that you can't do for yourself, due to your confinement."

The djinn paused to reflect. "AHH, HEE, HAH! There IS something you can do, to entertain me. The agreement with Gaea is that we are to be granted extraordinary powers in order for us to assist others. To ensure our assistance we are genetically coerced to help those worthy of it. That statement is open to interpretation, so Gaea has mandated we are to help those who have helped us. In return for the assistance, we must grant them one wish, anything they desire that is within our power to give. What would be entertaining to me is for you to assist my friend Skink, a djinn detained within Coal Pyramid. Lord Coal provided him a venue for study. In exchange, Skink owes him one wish. Lord Coal hasn't yet decided what that wish is to be, so Skink remains under house arrest until a decision is reached. Lord Coal is a crafty one, and mean spirited. When he dies---the sooner the better---he'll certainly be re-created as a djinn."

"So you wish us to free this Skink?" asked Centaur.

"Yes, but in doing so Skink will be indebted to you."

"Where is he held?" asked Pulp.

"In the dungeon, of course. You wouldn't want a djinn to be free to interact with people that might do a good deed for him? Their wish would trump Lord Coal's."

The salt djinn guffawed once more before melting back into a puddle, then draining into the ground. I shook my head. "Is everything in the Negative Frontier going to be this stupid?"

"Huh," muttered Centaur.

"Never mind."

We had to stop two more times, to collect elem fiero. The delay wasn't welcomed, but Dinga pleaded. "How long might it be before we travelled to another desert?" She had a point. Our enthusiasm for deserts had waned. We had no intention of returning to one unless it was absolutely necessary.

Chapter 19

BRIMSTONE

The pyramid the djinn spoke of was centered in an oasis. The structure was twice the height of the surrounding palms. Meters within the foliage five red dogs with black eyes assailed us. We---meaning my companions---instinctively went into a defensive stance. I had ruptured the orb, but I didn't intend to make violence, initiated by myself, or against my person, a routine. It wasn't that I was opposed to it, but as a spectator. I preferred not to dirty myself, unless it was---absolutely---necessary.

The dogs ran past us to chase a family of meerkats. Predator closed in on prey, but a burrow was just ahead. The meerkats were going to make it. The dogs stopped. It wasn't like canines to give up so easily, even with almost certain defeat glaring at them. They opened their mouths. Flames shot out, striking the meerkats, who were just a lunge from safety. They were blown over, then set ablaze. Still smoking, the meerkats were consumed.

"Dog eat cat," said Pulp.

"You think they may have left one of them behind?" asked General Paint.

"You still hungry?" asked Centaur. "You ate half of our rations. What remains needs to last until we reach Blowing Sand."

Dinga crinkled her nose.

"I've changed my mind," the trog blurted.

"That rotten egg smell is sulphur, also known as brimstone," Dinga elucidated. "The dogs must create it somehow, using it as a component for the flames they dispel."

"So we're going to have to smell more of that when we fight

the dogs?" Smells were different underground: more earthy, less floral, and most importantly, less extreme. In time, General Paint became acclimated, but not entirely.

"Who says we have to fight them. Dogs are pack animals. They become aggressive when their pack is overwhelmingly strong. We're too powerful, and numerous, to attack."

One of the flame-dogs did what dogs do in public. The stool turned to flames as soon as it was oxygenated. A small piece of charcoal hit the ground.

"That's the way to do it," said Pulp.

We entered the oasis jungle, our eyes on the flame-dogs as we made our way to the pyramid. They followed us, periodically snarling, exposing their black gums and their needle-sharp canines, but they kept their distance.

Half a kay into the jungle we entered a clearing. The odor of the dogs' discharge was potpourri compared to what we now smelled. General Paint vomited.

"That's going to help," uttered Pulp, wryly.

"Don't expect a replacement," said Centaur. "You're still not getting any more food until we reach Blowing Sand."

A rocky mound jutted into the sky. Steam and hot water spit out of its multiple fissures. On top of the mound was the pyramid. It was 50 meters high, nearly as tall as the mound. The runoff from the hot springs formed a moat around the raised earth. An eel swam in it. Either the water wasn't as hot as we believed it to be, or the eel had re-creationally adapted. Additional pools pocketed the clearing. They varied in color, from almost black, to brown, red, orange, yellow, green, and blue.

"Would I be correct to assume the moat wouldn't be safe to cross?" asked Centaur.

"Your clothes would become clean," said Pulp. "And given enough time your meat would come cleanly off your bones."

"There's a cave over there," I said.

"And isn't that a drawbridge?" questioned Hornet. "But it's up."

"Do we just knock?" asked Centaur.

"I've always used a transport portal to enter Coal's keep," stated Pulp. "I never entered the pyramid from the oasis. If Coal wished us to enter I believe the drawbridge would already be down. I guess it's time to begin sucking up: ALL MIGHTY COAL, LET US IN! YOU KNOW WE'RE HERE!"

A moment later, a...mummy?...appeared in the opening of the cave. It began to unwrap itself. The cloth had words on it. Pulp snagged the end of it once it dropped low enough for him to reach. He read: "If it's that important to you to enter the pyramid, you will find a way. I'll be beyond the bull."

"That's unlikely," Pulp added under his breath. The cloth scroll rose as the mummy rewrapped. It reentered the cave. Before it repaired itself a hollow space had been exposed beneath the cloth strips, not the preserved corpse normally associated with mummies.

"How does Lord Coal command the Dead?" asked Hornet. "Does it have something to do with him living in the Negative Frontier?"

"It wasn't really dead," I explained. "It was more like a golem---a construct---but without a soul. The mummy was simply an animated object. It looked like the cloth itself was what was animated. True Dead have souls. They are partial re-creations. Something goes wrong after they die and only part of them returns alive. Skeletons and zombies are animated objects. Ghouls are rotting corpses that are still partially alive. How would you like it if your flesh was decaying and falling off in pieces? Dead are never in a good mood. It's merciful to kill them, but not very effective. Once a person is damned, it's unlikely they will ever be re-created normally again."

"So that mummy was created by a Wizard?" asked Centaur.

"But probably not directly. Gents and Wizards don't get along. Coal likely bought a device that does the animating for him."

"What did the cloth mean by BEHIND THE BULL?" asked Dinga.

"Coal likes competitions. He creates contests of physical

and mental skill, watching when he doesn't participate in them himself. He creates puzzles and physical obstacles to challenge his guests."

"That seems to be a common theme around here," said Hornet.

"Do we have to go through with it?" asked Centaur. "It's like one of those challenges associated with finding a sphere, but without the treasure at the end. Is it worth the hassle? Can't we just take the elem and leave?"

"Coal has more than fire-hounds and mummies at his disposal," said Pulp. "If we succeed he will allow us to take the elem. He is ordered, negatively ordered, but still ordered. Before we reconstruct the portal it's likely we'll have to travel to Chaneg. We can expect no honor there."

"We should implement Pulp's advice," said Dinga. "In the time it takes to find elem terra---and I wish to find at least two, so we can stockpile a reserve---Lord Coal could create substantial mischief. How long might it take to prospect our own? I haven't spotted any elem yet. And I'm getting to where I can sense its general location. This oasis is relatively small, and surrounded by an elem void. Given time I ought to be able to find at least one elem, but I need that time."

"I believe your assistance is needed to circumvent our first obstacle, Lady Dinga," I said. I'm not without patience. It's just limited when I know we need to be doing something and no one else seems to care.

"Oh." Dinga sounded surprised, then embarrassed. Hornet used a blanket as a curtain. Dinga undressed. As he dropped the blanket, a raven flew away, over the moat, retaining enough altitude to prevent it from getting scalded by the fiery moat. Dinga waddled into the cave. A steel bridge lowered to our side of the moat.

We scrutinized the bubbling liquid below through the steel mesh walkway. I couldn't feel the heat, but the reactions of my companions told me they could. Their exit off the bridge was as much of a leap as a step.

The fire-hounds trotted off, back towards the perimeter of the oasis. One of them coughed, forcing out an unplanned burst of flame.

Hornet held up the blanket again as Dinga dressed. Was it inconsistent for someone who had been a prostitute to be concerned with states of undress, her own in particular? But be it motherhood or moral revelation, Dinga now preferred nudity to be a solitary experience.

"You sure you won't reconsider your decision to return to Berry?" asked General Paint.

"I've made up my mind. The uncertainty is how it's going to happen. Not travelling by ship limits my options. You wouldn't happen to have any friends nearby, Nimbus?"

"Friends? No." The last thing I wanted to do was meet another drak, especially one living in the Negative Frontier. The best way to divert attention from uncomfortable situations was to change the subject. "General Paint, I believe it is now your turn to impress us."

"The effects of the enfeeblement have diminished, but they haven't completely left my system. Let's see what I remember about stone and dirt." The trog proudly walked in front of us. He felt useful again. How belittling it must have felt being a warrior's warrior and not being able to fight, due to a mental injury. And before that he had relegated himself to being our bodyguard, after being the commander of Limbo's most powerful army. I felt much affinity for the trog. If he could return to importance, albeit in a limited capacity, for a limited period, I could too. I have helped out some lately, haven't I? Leadership is overrated. I was too limited in what I could do as mayor of Lizard Falls.

"Tunnels catacomb the pyramid and beneath it," stated General Paint. "Would Lord Coal put himself atop the pyramid, or far below it?"

"The djinn is supposedly in the dungeon," said Dinga. "If we free it, couldn't we ask it for elem terra as our reward?"

"Dungeon's are usually down," said Hornet.

86

"So there's a possibility we may not actually have to meet Lord Coal?" Centaur commented.

"Don't count on it," said Pulp. "Coal didn't go through all this effort to have visitors bypass his labyrinth."

Chapter 20

SHIFTING

"This way will lead down," General Paint declared. We followed the trog though the twisting maze of stone and earth. Sometimes we went down, other times up, but accumulatively, more down. Scones lit the tunnels, glowing red, likely from glow beetles, like the trogs used. We came to a dozen forks, but somehow General Paint always knew which way to go. The tunnels began to get warmer. A burst of hot air flowed past us, suffocating in its intensity.

"Are we almost there?" asked Dinga. "Be it my pregnancy, or my wimpiness, I can't take much more."

"We've dropped 83 meters since entering the cave," stated General Paint.

"If the pyramid and mound were inverted, how far from the top would we be?" asked Centaur.

"About 10 meters," I answered. "A valid theory. If Coal is highly ordered---and those living in the Ordered Frontier run the spectrum, from nearly neutral to exceedingly anal---it's likely he would make the depth of his keep the same as its height."

The furnace became more intense---and brighter. A cavern opened in front of us. Hot air rushed past us, up the narrow corridor behind.

"What are they?" Dinga was referring to the 150 sim salamanders that stood on their hind legs. They carried metal spears. The remains of many creatures lay before them. The salamanders glowed red, like metal in fire. My companions perspired profusely. Sweat beaded on their arms and foreheads.

One of the salamanders threw its spear. It struck Pulp's blackened arm, melting through it like it was made of butter. The gent grimaced, not from the contact with his dead flesh, but from the peripheral heat. "It's as hot as a branding iron."

The other three salamanders threw their spears. Aware now what they were capable of, my companions brought their shields out in front of them. The hot rods bounced safely off them, landing with clanks onto the stone ground. The salamanders scuttled towards us. We released arrows. They struck the salamanders, briefly knocking them backwards before the wooden shafts caught fire. The wounds we inflicted must have been superficial, because they kept coming.

We backed up into the tunnel. What would my existence be like if my wooden extremities burned? Would I still exist as just a rocky top? Would I finally die? But I wouldn't return as a drak. Or would I? If I wasn't a drak when I died was there the possibility I could be re-created into one.

"How do we destroy fire?" asked Centaur. "I would consider fleeing, but that's not an option if we want to find Skink---unless there's another route." He looked at General Paint.

The trog shook his head. A moment later he smiled. "But we could build one."

"How long would that take?"

"A couple of weeks."

"It would take two weeks for a trog to dig a few meters around a cave?"

"I thought you meant all the way to the djinn. A detour would take a day, or two, if we had the proper equipment."

"Do we?"

"Well, no. I guess I got so caught up in the moment I didn't think it through. Ah, childhood memories." When General Paint referred to his childhood, it was in reference to being a trog, those initial years when everything felt unfamiliar, but exciting. Children aren't born on Limbo, and adults don't age, not noticeably. Being new to a mutant form feels like starting over. It takes years for a person to become comfortable in their skin again---or hide or scales....

"So trogs dig for fun?" questioned Dinga. "Instead of playing ball, or cards?"

"Well, when one first becomes a trog they have this itch to borrow. It takes a few years to get it out of our system. I guess we never completely do. Those who have chosen a career in borrowing are considered juvenile, wasting their lives PLAYING. They are envied, though. Ah, to have the luxury of living a leisurely lifestyle."

"Someone has to do it, don't they? To repair dilapidated tunnels and build new ones."

"True. Trogs also have this need to sacrifice for the collective. Living underground we must rely on one another to survive. The more we sacrifice the more patriotic we become. I made the greatest of sacrifices running off with you."

"We appreciate your...sacrifice."

"I don't feel that way anymore. Being part of a collective we become homesick easily. It's difficult spending the entire day in the field, so most don't, returning home for lunch, more for psychological nourishment than from the food we eat."

"But trogs do travel sometimes," I insisted.

"Not often. Wanderlust is a disease, those inflicted quarantined to preserve the realm."

After a moment to digest what General Paint said, Hornet made a suggestion. "We could smother them. We do that to campfires when we don't have time for them to burn themselves out on their own."

"Good idea, but what can we smother them with? You don't suggest we do it with our bodies."

"Water," I proposed.

"We don't have enough," said Centaur.

"I might be able to create some," said Dinga. We climbed an additional 20 meters up the passage, giving us a few extra seconds to react if the salamanders attacked again.

Dinga removed an elem extractor and discharged it five times into the makeshift water basin. By the time she stirred it, the salamanders were five meters away. She flung the water at them, coming up short. As soon as it hit the ground, the pool it formed doubled in volume, then doubled again. When the salamanders stepped into it, they sizzled. Steam rose. They panicked. They fled, in the direction they came. The water continued to multiply. A trickle of water flowed downhill, then a steady stream, then a torrent. Abruptly, the water ceased flowing. Without a source the stream became a trickle again, and finally just wet ground. We cautiously walked downhill. All of us slipped at least once, including me. The water pooled in the cavern. It was noticeably cooler. Four worms floated in the knee deep pool that was slowly draining into the porous ground.

"Heat without much substance, like an animal that puffs itself up to appear more powerful," I commented. "There is a possibility they might revive, but not soon, hours, if not days away."

"They look dead to me," said Hornet.

"As they do to me. It was only a possibility."

A tunnel at the back of the cavern led to a cell block. A gray replica of the sand djinn was its only occupant.

"Skink, I presume," said Pulp.

"It's about time," it said. "I've been stuck down here for...too long. Lord Coal will now wish he used his wish instead of hoarding it. If something sits long enough it will eventually spoil. A lost opportunity for enjoyment before I ruin it."

"I didn't think a djinn could take revenge upon someone he traded favors with," spoke Centaur.

"If you free me from my obligation to Lord Coal, I won't be committing revenge upon someone I assisted, because I wouldn't have had the opportunity to assist him."

"We wish...." began Dinga.

90

"Caution," I reminded.

"We wish...."

The djinn sighed. "You need to free me first."

General Paint struck the lock repeatedly until it broke. "Couldn't you have just opened this yourself?" he asked.

"Micro-man, the cage was symbolic. Lord Coal could have drawn a line around me and I wouldn't be able to cross it." The stone djinn walked out of the cell. "Now that you have so generously freed me, what can I do for you in return?" If it had spoken with less emotion we would have fallen asleep.

"Now," I spoke to Dinga.

"We wish you to collect all the elem terra in the oasis surrounding Lord Coal's keep, as quickly as possible." Just before it vanished, Dinga added, "You are to give us the elem when you're done."

"It was in a hurry, wasn't it," said Centaur.

"The sooner it completes its task, the sooner it can get on with its life," I said. "The same could be said for us."

"Let's try to leave," said Centaur. "We don't know if we can't until we try."

We walked back up the passageway. It was still slippery, forcing us to do so slowly, with caution.

General Paint stopped abruptly. "The catacombs have been altered. There is no longer an outlet."

"The old shifting passage trick," said Hornet.

"Is there still an outlet somewhere?" asked Centaur. "Or are you finally given the opportunity to relive your youth?"

"There is an outlet, but there's no direct route to it."

"Of course," said Pulp. "We haven't experienced all that Coal has to offer."

"Lead on, General Paint," said Centaur.

"DUCK!" General Paint shouted minutes into our roundabout excursion. A score of crossbow bolts were discharged from the wall. If it wasn't for the warning, most of us would have been skewered.

"Was that the equivalent of salamanders in this part of the

catacombs?" asked Centaur.

"There's movement ahead," said General Paint.

"That answers that question."

A cavern about the size of the salamanders' opened up. A five-meter tall humanoid with a bull's head blocked the tunnel behind it. It grasped tightly a double-edged battle axe. The weapon was massive, almost as large as the thing that held it.

"Together we should be able to defeat it," said Hornet.

"It might be easier than that," said Dinga. "Look closely at its legs. They're chained."

"It doesn't want to be here anymore than we do," I stated. "Look at the pleading in its eyes. It doesn't care if it wins. If we kill it, it will be re-created, freeing it from Lord Coal's pyramid."

"THEN ALLOW ME TO ASSIST IT!" said General Paint. "I have more than enough motivation to be victorious." The trog rushed it. He looked comical, a small dog nipping at someone's feet. The creature had two perceptible weaknesses. The first: its armor was leather. From the look of it, of human origin. Not human-made, but made out of humans. The second: its speed. A creature that large couldn't swing a proportional weapon fast enough to be effective against a much smaller opponent.

The trog struck many times, often disregarding his own safety in order to get one more attack in. His considerable advantage in quickness enabled him to flawlessly dodge the axe. The creature's multiple wounds dripped large ochre drops. The loss of blood was beginning to take its toll. The creature was weakening. Before finally being defeated by his more motivated opponent, it struck General Paint soundly between his shoulder and chest. The plate mail was dented, but not penetrated. The trog fell to the ground. He came out of his daze just in time to roll away from being struck in the head. Without getting up, General Paint swung his axe, clipping both of the creature's legs. It fell forward, barely missing the trog. General Paint, with surprising agility, jumped up and chopped at it manically, like he was making kindling.

Dinga examined the trog. He winced as she put pressure in

the vicinity of the indentation. "It may be just a bruise, but I think you have a couple of broken ribs, and possibly internal injuries. You'll need a flesh healing elixir as soon as the djinn returns with elem terra."

Chapter 21

ARENA

The tunnel the bull guarded angled-up, steeply. Light shined brightly down it, with an intensity associated with sunlight. We entered the ground level of a coliseum. It was square, with meter-high terraces, nine total, climbing to the top. We had made it to the top of the pyramid.

Sitting on a chair in proportion to his six meter height was a dark-skinned man with red hair and beard. He wore bronze armor over his upper torso. He sat halfway up the terraces, his chair on top of a track. Four mummies, two on each side, pulled the chair with ropes.

At the far end of the field, a winged lion was being attacked by five mummies and two flame-hounds.

A stone block fell, blocking our exit.

The winged lion must have had its wings clipped, because it couldn't fly more than a few meters before falling back down. The mummies, not being able to think for themselves, attacked with little imagination. They ran towards the lion, attempting to tackle it. Their weight was so insignificant, in comparison to the lion's, the lion barely budged. One of the mummies tried to choke it---a far better tactic when one was made of cloth---but the lion countered by raising a claw, ripping the cloth arms away. The mummies were better at defense, particularly when grouped together clasping appendages. Their elasticity repelled the lion, flinging it backwards whenever it pounced on them.

The flame-hounds were more effective. While one distracted the winged lion, the other either blew flames at it, singing its fur, or bit it.

After the initial skirmishes the mummies and flame-hounds began to work together. As the mummies corralled the flying lion, the flame-hounds attacked simultaneously from behind. The only direction the lion could move was towards the hounds. They both must have recharged their fire, because after digging in with their teeth, they flamed the lion at point blank range. The immolation spread rapidly, the two small fires merging into one larger fire. The flame-hounds held on. They prevented the lion from rolling over, which may have put out the fire prematurely. After the fire had burnt a majority of its body, the dogs let go. The lion gave one last roar, then toppled. With its fuel source expiring, the fire began to diminish.

There were dozens of spectators sitting on the terraces. All were human, except for a small gent in very ragged clothes, and a reptilian hybrid. They cheered enthusiastically when the lion caught on fire. They stopped when the creature had stopped moving.

The dark gent hit a gong attached to his chair. Opposite sides of the arena opened. The mummies left through one of the openings. The flame-hounds through the other.

Pulp walked forward, towards the gent. We followed him. He stopped three-quarters of the way across the field, about 20 meters from the beginning of the terrace.

"Pulp, so nice of you to visit me," spoke the gent.

"A minotaur at the end of a maze. How clever."

"You use what you got. It didn't wish to fight, but I didn't want to waste such a magnificent creature, so it was given guard duty."

"The last time I was here YOU fought."

"It became too easy."

"That's because you gave yourself unfair advantages."

"You don't expect me to get myself killed after all I have achieved?"

"And didn't you use to have a game with rules?"

"The game just got in the way. People come to the arena to see the fights, not to see who can score the most points. I decided to skip all that boring stuff."

"The winged lion volunteered?"

"Some of my participants had a bit of a motivation problem. Freedom as a reward for winning works most of the time. I should have been a coach."

"Wasn't doing something like this the reason you were sentenced to Limbo?"

"Paying homeless people to fight one another. They chose to participate, but the law abused their civil rights by making the competitions illegal. Then they took away my civil rights by incarcerating me."

"You release your participants if they win?"

"You don't see me living in the South, do you?" He was referring to the Chaotic Frontier.

"Are we to be your next participants?"

"You know I can't harm you, but if you volunteered to assist your companions---and they'll certainly need it---I won't forbid it." Lord Coal noticed my arm. "Perhaps, I overstated your potential contribution to their wellbeing. I may be willing to make a deal, say, your vote at the next Brotherhood Council. I believe we were dead-locked the last time we voted."

Before Pulp could respond Centaur pulled him back towards us. We huddled together. "You don't need to relinquish your morals, Pulp. That's why you dreaded coming here. You knew Lord Coal would make this offer."

"I knew the offer would be made, but I still came. Saving the four of you would be worth it. I have pondered long and hard. The debate of all debates: should the Brotherhood take a larger role in Limboan politics. The Wizards' power must be countered, but are two competing global powers better than one? What is the lesser of the two evils?"

"If Lord Coal wants you to do this, doesn't that tell you something?" asked Dinga.

"Just because an evil person believes something doesn't make it wrong---invalidate the belief. Is it wrong for a murderer to feed the poor?"

"Do you wish Lord Coal to change your mind?" I asked.

"I must decline his offer, mustn't I?"

Pulp broke from the huddle and walked toward the moving chair. "I will not change my vote."

"Then decide hastily: participant or spectator? Your opponents will be arriving in one minute." Lord Coal hit the gong. Three breaches appeared at the perimeter of the arena.

"Reputation of my affluence must be spreading. I've never had a gent attempt to steal from me before. But with honey comes the sting. I've added one more group to my army of entertainers. They cost me dearly, but I now have the resources, thanks to healthy contributions from my patrons."

Ten mummies and four flame-hounds emerged from the apertures---and three gargoyles. The latter group immediately flew to the top of the arena.

"Maybe we can just climb out of here," Hornet suggested.

"Try," Pulp countered. When Hornet came within a step of the terraces, three levels moved away from him, forming a four-meter tall shear wall.

We clustered, facing outward. The maneuvering against us was similar to the attack against the lion. The mummies rushed us in an attempt to get close enough to strangle us, while the hounds worked together to distract us, so they could sneak in a surprise attack. To counter the maneuver, we watched all directions simultaneously, while knocking or cutting away all cloth arms within our reach. The disadvantage of us being so close together was an attack on one of us meant an attack on all. We learned that the hard way when we were first flamed by a hound. We developed a communication system. With practice we were able to move in sync at an instant's notice.

We used the tactic to great effect, one time in particular. When two of the flame-hounds blew fire at us from two different directions, we were able to dodge the attack at the last moment. The mummies beside us not having the wits to move out of the way were less fortunate. Dry cloth encasing oxygenated air was a volatile mix. That got a reaction from the crowd, who hadn't been too enthusiastic up to that point, because we hadn't been critically injured---yet. Didn't anyone rout for the underdog anymore?

If it wasn't for the gargoyles, we may have been victorious. They attacked with talons and teeth from above. We couldn't monitor our perimeter and our ceiling simultaneously. We were so involved in defending ourselves we had forgotten the flyers, who hadn't yet attacked us. Pulp, being the tallest of us, by far, received the majority of the scratches. A couple of centimeters more to the left and he would have lost an eye. With us being distracted now, the mummy and flame-hound attacks became more successful. The mummies moved us about, improving the precision of the flame-hound attacks. Everyone but Hornet had at least second degree burns. My arms were blackened, but not deep enough to cause structural damage. Even with all the---often painful---mischief the mummies and flame-hounds were creating, we were more troubled by the gargoyles. They were learning from their mistakes---and ours. They waited for the precise moment to strike, as we defended ourselves from our other assailants.

"The gargoyles are real," I enlightened. "They're not animated objects. They must have been created with black elem---elem essence." There have been rumors of people harvesting souls for decades. It's been hypothesized that a person's essence, their soul, is a complex bundle of energy. Elem are also bundles of energy. Could a soul then be able to replace elem in a penta? If it could, life could be re-created in any form the possessor of the penta wished, dependent on the vessel prepared. I'm living proof that black elem exists. If we are able to create life, are we competing with Gaea? Are we playing God?

As usual, Hornet rarely got hit. Those rare times he did it was usually as secondary damage from the person beside him. The GRACE OF GAEA continued to protect him, and to a lesser degree, us, as a peripheral effect. Sometimes it worked against us, a stray blow having to go somewhere.

The sky darkened. Was it an omen, or just our enthusiasm waning? No matter, the inevitable end was near.

A dust storm entered the arena. So jarring was its unanticipated approach, the flame-hounds and gargoyles ceased attacking. The latter even sat down on the far side of the field, not wishing to fly in the debris. The wind concentrated into a dust devil. It headed towards us. As it reached the ground it became even more concentrated, shrinking as it became more dense. The stone djinn materialized.

It opened one hand. Four glowing green specs were in it. Dinga extracted them with an elem collector. "Free at last." The djinn grinned wickedly.

It walked up the terrace steps, its legs long enough to do so without climbing or leaping---after cresting the initial stacked steps. "I won't be as rude as you," the djinn spoke to Lord Coal. "I won't make you wait before I enact my revenge."

Chapter 22

CASHING IN

We didn't wait to see the outcome of the battle. We climbed the terraces, then down the other side onto the pyramid's exterior. Being too short to pull myself up Pulp had to tuck me under one arm. At the base of the pyramid the billowing gases and liquids caused us some concern. But through trial and error---many errors---we negotiated a safe route around them. After crossing the drawbridge, we made an accelerated effort to leave the oasis. The flame-hounds were noticeably absent, being either inside the pyramid, or, our preferred explanation, the stone djinn had destroyed them while collecting elem terra.

We walked until we felt safe to stop---more than half an hour later. "Time to fix that arm," said Dinga. She swirled four elem aqua with a single elem terra. The color changed to a dark sea green. The elixir was handed to Pulp. He consumed it in one swallow. Nothing happened.

"You don't think that djinn deceived us?" Centaur commented.

"Technically, no," I replied. "It was under contract to provide all the elem terra within the oasis. There may have been none and it substituted a placebo."

"Could it be that cruel?" Dinga asked.

"Yes, but the question we should be asking is WOULD IT?"

After a brief pause Hornet said, "No. It was too focused on Lord Coal. Cunning is time consuming."

"IT'S BEGINNING TO WORK!" Dinga shouted.

Pulp's blackened arm began oozing puss. It coated his arm like perspiration. The concentration of it eventually built up enough to merge into a single mass. It began to harden and turn pink. Minute cracks began to form. Fingernails grew, as did hair.

Pulp's face began to whiten. He would have fallen if Centaur and Hornet hadn't caught him. "What's wrong?" asked Centaur.

"Healing this much tissue takes its toll," said Dinga. "Give him some food. That will help. He'll also need sleep."

"Now? We need to put more distance between us and that pyramid before we bed down for the night."

"We'll see how he does after he eats. It may revive him enough to travel another hour or more."

The food did help. Pulp was still weak, but not weak enough that he couldn't walk.

We returned to the salt flats. My companions preferred to detour around them. "We need to meet the bronze djinn again," I insisted, but didn't elaborate.

He materialized in front of us. "Did you chicken out, or did you actually…. Ah, hee, hah. The gent has been healed. Did you also free Skink?"

"He is playing with Lord Coal," said Centaur. "I don't think he'll play nicely."

"Skink never was very social. Have you returned to gloat? A great error on your part. Amusing a djinn once---rare. Amusing one twice…ah…."

"Raw?" I threw out.

"I like you, Sticks-and-Stones. With much regret I'll have to come up with something nasty to do to you and your fleshier companions."

"HEY!" Dinga instinctively blurted.

"I'm certain the flesh on you is in the right places, madam. It does seem to be a bit superfluous though, don't you think?"

"HEY!"

"My meaning is it isn't necessary on Limbo. It gets in the way. It burns. It scratches. It moves too much."

"HEY!"

Well, this is getting redundant. Time to return to the task. "Why are you stuck here, in these salt flats, while Skink can travel where he wishes?" I asked.

"Excellent question. And to answer it simply: Skink can't. To limit a djinn's power Gaea limit's its habitat."

I just noticed something. The djinn refers to its kind as an it, not a he or a she. Does it consider itself asexual? FEEK! Now that I think about it, I haven't thought about women---females of any species---since I became a golem. Elementals, of one variety or another, must be of one gender. When I'm re-created into another form will I be male again? Will I remain asexual? Or is there a possibility I might even become female? From neutral one can either shift into drive or reverse.

Back to the djinn. "Skink's current habitat is the Pyramid Oasis. He and Lord Coal must be having the time of their lives. When someone is granted a wish, that person controls where the djinn's base of operation is. If the djinn is commanded to go somewhere, it does. Once the wish it successfully granted, the djinn's current location becomes its new habitat."

"I would like to cash in a wish."

"But…. Hee haw. Of course. Crafty is the once-powerful once-drak."

I explained. "The bronze djinn wanted us to free Skink. By doing so, we did him a favor. Dinga, this is your opportunity to return to Berry, quickly, and without having to travel by ship."

She looked like she was about to change her mind again. She hugged Hornet, nearly squeezing him to death. Then she kissed him expeditiously. "Take these elem collectors. Remember to use four elem aqua for all healing elixirs. Add an elem terra to heal the flesh, a elem fiero to cure a disease, and an elem aero to return energy. Gaea-willing, I will see you all again. Will you be back to Berry in time to see your son or daughter being born?"

"Gaea-willing, sooner." Hornet kissed Dinga one last time.

"Transport Dinga to…wait." I almost made a tragic mistake. "Transport Dinga five kays south of Berry."

I expected the djinn to carry Dinga away in a cloud of dust or something. They simply disappeared. What power the djinn must have at their disposal, to travel anywhere on Limbo instantaneously. Without constraints what might they be capable of?

"Can you imagine the mischief the djinn might create inside a city?" I elaborated.

"Is Dinga going to be alright?" asked Hornet.

"The djinn won't harm her. She can make it the rest of the way to Berry---safely---on her own. After that the Healer will help her. Her anguish will be thinking about us. The skin of the Negative Frontier is much safer than its heart."

We were motivated to travel until sundim. We didn't wish to remain in the salt flats, even with the djinn no longer present.

Putting more distance between us and the oasis wouldn't hurt. We hoped to reach the creek before dark. We didn't make it. We were determined to before stopping, so we continued on in the dim light. The moon wasn't bright enough for us to read, but we could walk. There weren't any trees or hills in the desert to obstruct its illumination. It would have been even brighter if we weren't so far from the orb, the Frontier being on the rim of Limbo.

"We shouldn't be traveling in the dark," Pulp cautioned. "This is the time the Dead come out. I'd feel safer beside a campfire."

"You just got done fighting more than a dozen monsters with claws and teeth, and flame, and you are afraid of transparent spooks?" Centaur questioned.

"They are more than that. Ghouls are the walking dead. They reek of decomposing flesh. They make you want to turn your insides out, struggling to vomit. If they touch you that odor is harder to get rid of than skunk. Ghosts are ethereal. They can pass through you. It feels like ants are crawling on you, but from the inside. They also transmit thoughts to you, memories of their sorrows, including their death. Then there are wraiths. They are the worst, because they are the most deadly. They capture souls, like an elem collector captures elemental energy. After the soul is stolen its body dies, but something prevents the soul from surrounding itself with a re-creation. The wraith controls the soul. The soul can sense what is occurring, but as a spectator. The energy associated with the soul gradually draws in dust particles, like an electromagnetic field. A dark cloud is formed. Ultimately the tie to the original wraith is broken. By this time, many months later, the hate it feels for its captor, itself, the universe, has built up to irrational proportions. The newly formed wraith, like an abused child, wants to do to others what was done to it, perpetuating the cycle."

"And the Dead just wander aimlessly in the dark?" Hornet asked.

"They have a goal: to seek others to torment."

"Maybe we should set up camp, now," Centaur suggested. "A fire keeps them away?"

"Usually, especially the ghouls. The only way to destroy them is with fire. If their flesh is gone, the soul has nothing to cling to, so it is set free, either to inhabit another corpse, or on rare occasions, to share a re-created body."

"Ghouls are never re-created?" asked Hornet. "Are they doomed to eternal torment?"

"Supposedly."

"In those cases it's best just to die," commented Pulp. "But Gaea, Limbo, the creators of this prison, won't let this happen, will they?"

"You've lived as long as you wish to?" asked Centaur.

"Not as long as women are re-created into arbols."

"What makes arbol women so great? Women are women, aren't they?"

"Women are more uninhibited in the Chaotic Frontier. Gaea adapted arbols to live in trees. They are extremely limber, putting the most gifted gymnasts to shame."

Ah, the memories. Women tended to gravitate to powerful men, so I had more than my fair share. The kind of women who liked men like me were more trophy than companion, but it would have been rude not to take what one was offered.

"Ghosts are powerless in bright light," Pulp continued. "A nearby fire is sufficient to keep them away. Too bright a light is said to kill them. Not sure if it's the light or the energy behind it. Ghosts rarely venture out in a lightning storm. Close proximity to a lightning strike always destroys them."

"How about wraiths?" asked Centaur.

"Wraiths are difficult to destroy, and fire doesn't always keep them away. They are attracted to the smoke. The debris in it they devour to make themselves larger. The fire itself they don't like, because it can burn their debris cloud, consuming it."

"So wraiths are attracted to smoky fires, but won't actually attack you if you're near one? That won't make for a restful sleep."

"Or a trip to the bathroom in the middle of the night,"

Hornet added. "How do we kill one?"

"I've never heard of anyone actually doing so."

"I have a theory," I volunteered. "When you live decades one has time to develop many theories." Yes, I have also heard of the Dead. Being a drak, though, they weren't considered to be dangerous, just a novelty. "There aren't any wraiths in arctic regions. There isn't much of anything in those areas, but I think the cold is particularly hard on them. I believe it has to do with their magnetic fields. Cold slows things down, including electrons. If a wraith can be frozen, not just to zero, but significantly below that, it might be destroyed. It's just a theory. The best way to keep all Dead away is to stay in a well-lit area. Even wraiths don't like the conflicting energies. That is one reason Dead aren't common in cities. There are always light boundaries somewhere. They act as walls to the Dead. In the wild there are fewer boundaries."

We intersected the road beside the creek about the time we had scared ourselves enough that we would have made camp no matter where we were. If it wasn't for the creek---trees grew beside water---we wouldn't have had enough fuel to build a fire. Even more difficult would have been sustaining it. The cottonwoods dropped enough branches for us to build a fire ring around us. It had a few gaps, but they weren't large enough for anything man-size to squeeze through. Were we excessive? Yes. Excessive for our protection, possibly, but not for our psyches. I wasn't worried for myself. What could the Dead do to a golem? But I did have companions now, who I would even call friends. Were they my first? My relationships with people had varied in how I could use them. Did the correctional system actually work? For me, perhaps. Might other government systems also work, then? Might I actually have a future now, if I left Limbo---if I was able to return to my original form? Was I really contemplating working for the government? That would be the greatest of challenges: managing the universe, not just for my benefit, but for mankind's.

No spooks got through our defenses. None were even

spotted. I lot of worrying for nothing, but that was better than not worrying and having something dreadful happen to us.

Chapter 23

PRAYING

By late morning we began seeing signs of civilization: crops mainly, growing along the banks of Grit Creek. I didn't see any homes, but how many people living in the Negative Frontier would willingly abandon the safety of a city? Most of the farms employed beasts of burden, a taboo for Westerners and Centralists.

"I understand why it's frowned upon," Hornet commented, "but that's under the assumption that people are sometimes re-created as animals. Is there evidence of this ever happening?"

"Just because you haven't seen something happen doesn't mean it hasn't," General Paint responded. "There is no freewill without faith. Would you rather exist as a series of conditioned responses?"

"What you're proposing sounds very disorderly," said Pulp.

"There is a misconception that order is stagnant. To sustain order one must promote truth. The best way is by example. Truth is in flux, modified by condition and duration. Because it's snowing today doesn't mean it won't be sunny tomorrow."

"What purpose would there be in intentionally mutating someone into an animal? Beasts of burden already exist. Wouldn't it be redundant?"

"How often is spirituality, morals, religion, logical?" I questioned. "If they were, stagnation would occur, social, intellectual, and economical."

Blowing Sand's population---slightly less than a thousand---warranted it village status, but it looked more like a town because of how spread out it was. Large blocks were in a grid pattern centered at the intersection of the Norport and Jasper Highways, near the confluence of Grit Creek and the Serpent River. Cacti, scarce in Pyramid Sands, were plentiful in the village. Every business and home had at least one small cactus and rock garden.

The arts and crafts community, centered south of the village center, had some non-native trees and flowers, but it wasn't vast enough to distract from other areas of the village. A majority of the crafts were carvings, of animals and mutants, most recognizable. A few, not. The unfamiliar ones looked hazardous. It was likely, inevitable even, we would eventually meet them in the Negative Frontier.

Stucco was predominant. As were pools, private and public. With two major sources of water, rationing wasn't required.

Most of the residents wore clothing unfit for civilized society. Most, but not all. A quarter of the village's population was clothed in an overabundant manner. Robes, long stockings, and scarves covered them from head to tail. Masks concealed their countenances. Not a single hair or sim of skin was exposed. The masks they wore were without expression, as if displaying emotion was as scandalous as displaying flesh.

The largest building in Blowing Sand was THE THIRD TIME IS A CHARM CHURCH. It was in the northwest quadrant of the village center. The building was 100 meters tall, but most of that was a narrow cylindrical tower. The base of the building was bulbous, topped by four mounds. From a distance it looked like an apple. Two lines formed beside it: a single-file queue going into the building, another heading out.

"What do they believe?" asked Hornet.

"Primarily that being sent here, to Limbo, was divine intervention," Centaur explained. "If they weren't here they never would have felt the hand of Gaea as they were re-created. The THREE TIMES the church's name refers to is their life before incarceration, their life on Limbo, and their life after re-creation."

"They believe they are married to Gaea," Pulp added. "When she touched them to re-create them, they considered it to be not only spiritual, but sexual, a complete bonding experience. Not wanting to be unfaithful, they don't expose themselves physically, emotionally, or sexually to others."

"They truly believe they are able to make love to Gaea," I said. "Most of the space within a church is occupied by the private chambers its members use to get intimate with Gaea. I have no desire to even hypothesize what they might be doing in them. The tower is reserved for those married to Gaea the longest. If you look closely at the masks you'll notice small dots. Each represents an anniversary of their relationship with Gaea."

"Do they have a political agenda?" Hornet asked.

"Only in that they want everyone to be able to enjoy the private joy they feel in their relationship with Gaea," I said. "They do tend to be matchmakers. And because they are the ultimate married people, they usually only hang out with others married to Gaea, because they don't have much in common with those not making the commitment. If all were in such a healthy relationship, the world would be a much happier place."

"What happens if they are away from a church? Do they practice celibacy until they enter a settlement with a church?"

"Once a day they are required to make love to Gaea, to keep her happy," said Pulp. "If there isn't a church nearby they'll find a private place to worship. The MARRIED, as they call themselves, rarely travel. When they do it is to establish a new church in a settlement that doesn't have one."

We rented a room in an inn as far from The Third Time Is A Charm Church as we could. We preferred not to hear people PRAYING all night.

I didn't sleep. What would it be like to lose consciousness for two or three hours at a time? It's been so long I don't remember what sleeping was like. Because I didn't sleep I didn't dream. Did I miss out not being able to dream? How did it affect me psychologically not being able to set my consciousness free, to drain my thoughts? Is my subconscious getting full, like a septic tank on the brink of backing up?

What did I do while my companions slept? Guard duty, primarily. Boring? Yes, but more interesting than just standing there until they woke. But tonight, with them being in the protective embrace of a city, I abandoned them in order that I may explore. I had to be careful I didn't put myself in a position where I couldn't flee. A golem wasn't considered to be a sovereign entity. If I was captured, I would become slave labor.

The village was exceedingly calm: there were few sounds and trivial movement. I assumed a settlement this large in the Negative Frontier would be fairly active at night. The anomaly was resolved when I noticed a disproportionate number of patrolmen. The only way to survive in a dangerous environment was for there to be strict laws. One might even suggest overly strict. With a known reputation for lawfulness, fewer troublemakers would remain in the city. It was too much effort to rob or molest someone in a secure community. There were other opportunities, more welcoming settlements. With patrolmen everywhere, and no excitement to be had, I returned to the inn less than an hour later. My reconnaissance wasn't completely without profit. I found a store that sold penta. Blowing Sand wasn't large enough for an emporium---a Wizard-sponsored shop---but any venue that sold even a limited quantity of penta would be useful to us. We would need more than healing elixirs to survive in the Negative Frontier.

Chapter 24

SQUEAKS

"THESE PRICES ARE OUTRAGEOUS!" Centaur bellowed.

"This isn't an emporium," Pulp reminded him. "Second-hand sources are more expensive."

"We could create our own," Hornet suggested.

"Without Dinga here to guide us? Even Gaea won't be able to save you when it blows up in your face."

"Twelve gold sounds reasonable to me," said Pulp. "I've heard of prices twice that in remote areas."

"Blowing Sand isn't that remote."

"It's three days from Jasper."

Centaur looked in his wallet and frowned. He set aside half the coins, then counted. "We can buy three penta. How many of those ought to be for healing?"

"Can we afford to waste ANY on healing?" asked Pulp.

"For those of us who haven't been re-created a dozen times, we prefer to retain our current form as long as possible."

"A DOZEN TIMES?! I'm not THAT careless."

"I believe I can create healing elixirs," Hornet interjected. "I've seen Dinga do it."

"We all have, but that doesn't mean we can do it," said Centaur.

Time for my input. I spoke at a volume, and in a manner, the proprietor of the penta shop wouldn't notice. "We'll need more than healing elixirs to survive the Negative Frontier. Would it be wise to purchase something we may be able to produce?"

We determined LIGHTENING, COLD, and FIRE penta would be best. They were the most generic, the best use of our funds to counter diverse adversaries, many of them likely to be unknown.

Centaur turned towards General Paint after we exited the building. "You were awfully quiet in there."

"Trogs don't approve of witchcraft."

"Then why did you walk in?"

"To see if I could. Trogs may be concerned, but they aren't afraid."

"So we shouldn't have used penta to heal you," Hornet stated.

"Not approving doesn't mean we can't appreciate. Trogs prefer pummeling instead of slicing---it's less messy---but we won't complain if an expert swordsman fights beside us."

"Without Dinga here we'll be able to hire a ship to cross the Eastern Sea," said Centaur. "That ought to save us a week or more."

"You're that eager to enter the heart of the Negative Frontier?" asked Pulp.

"I'm that eager to leave it. Before we can leave we must arrive." Centaur removed the map of Limbo from his pack and examined it. "Norport is the closest port."

"But Jasper is larger," Pulp countered. "It will be easier to hire a ship there. If we head to Norport we may save a day walking, but in exchange for three or four waiting."

"Feek, can't any decision we make be simple?"

"Jasper is more cosmopolitan," Pulp enlightened.

"You miss seeing exotic women?"

"And other things."

"To Jasper we go." It may have soundly like Centaur had weighed all the variables and made a decision, but I think it had more to do with him being fed up with the arguing.

A citrus grove was discovered five kays south of the village. "Shall we supplement our provisions?" Pulp suggested.

"Does the utility warrant it?" I questioned. "In a harsh environment there are harsher penalties. Losing a piece of flesh equal in weight to the stolen item is a common practice."

"Do we get to choose what piece of flesh to lose?"

We followed the Serpent River for the entirety of the first day, spending the night in Scorpion, a lazy, dusty hamlet on the far shore. The bridge we crossed was dilapidated, surprising considering this was the only route to Jasper, the nexus for the settlement's livelihood, and basis for its existence. Why do something today when you can put it off until tomorrow? What a shock it was going to be to the community when it inevitably falls into the river. For every finger pointed there will be three targeting the cause.

The second night we spent in a way station. We shared its common room with four men. They looked alike. All had small, wiry frames, and beady, bloodshot eyes. They occupied two of the tables, and in the manner they were carrying on, they seemed to take up more space than that. Inns---including way stations---made their own beverages. Usually just ales, but sometimes brandies, whiskeys, even wines. The innkeeper was going to be busy restocking after the four men left. I made it a priority to never drink enough to impair my judgment. I didn't want to lose control. I didn't care if others drank. I even preferred it. It provided me a better opportunity to take advantage of them.

The four men were beginning to get to that point.

"Why don't we take the ring ourselves?" one of them asked with slurred speech. "Why must we wait for Emu to decide what to do?"

"Because Emu isn't an idiot," spoke another.

"Are you calling me an idiot?"

"An idiot can't help himself," spoke a third. "You're dumb by choice."

"Emu thinks we need more recruits," spoke the second again.

"The more involved, the smaller our cut."

"I'd rather give up a portion of my share than be killed, or captured. Becoming a beast of burden isn't much of a reprieve. Anarachs eat their slaves. When they don't have enough spoiled scraps to throw to them they encourage them to eat one another."

"Why so much planning? There is treasure everywhere." The pointy-nose men looked at us.

"Scat's right. Emu will take half the profit for himself. But what we...harvest...on our own...."

"Dung, what do you think will happen to us if Emu finds out we left his service?"

"We don't have to return to Jasper, Offal."

"And go where, Guano? Blowing Sand would lock us up within the first hour. You thinking about going cross-country? The Dead or something worse will find us before we reach the next town."

"What if we unite against Emu? If we took him out it would mean more money for us."

"Someone would just take his place."

"It might be me."

"Then how long would you live, with everyone trying to take your position away from you?"

"I still think we should go after the transport ring on our own."

"It's under the city. I'd rather have Emu leading us. He's been around longer than any of us. He'll know how to get the ring."

"Is everyone ready?" Centaur whispered. "I think it's time to return to our room."

We paid the innkeeper. "You may wish to secure your door extra tight tonight," he told us.

"Do you need our help?" asked Pulp.

"An innkeeper is as sacred as a priest to travelers. Reducing our livelihood, or terminating our lives, doesn't help anyone. Good evening."

Back in our room Centaur locked the door and placed a chair against its knob. He scanned the room. He paused at the window. He pushed the wardrobe in front of it, then one of the two double beds. "The only way they can come in now is with some elemental assistance, and they don't look like they can afford any."

"Should we make a detour before we travel across the Eastern Sea?" asked Hornet. "We've been underground before. How bad can these anarachs be?"

"What makes them dangerous is their xenophobia," Pulp explained. "They believe they are superior to...everyone. If it isn't possible to enslave another race, they'll destroy it. They feel it's their duty to cleanse the world of species that are unworthy."

"This transport ring they spoke of is an invaluable asset," I said. "It may be the only ring like it the Wizards don't possess. In fact, someone may have had to kill a Wizard to obtain it. The wearer of the ring will be able to travel instantaneously wherever he wishes within a certain range, the range depending on the ability of the user. There are limitations. A person must know the location he will be transported to. A mistake could mean rematerializing inside stone."

"Can we all be transported?"

"Potentially, but with a much greater risk. A cubic meter is easier to maneuver than two or three. And if anyone moves.... Like I said, it's possible, but not recommended."

"I vote we go after the ring," said Hornet.

"We still have three more spheres to find, and they all appear to be in the Negative Frontier," said Centaur. "We need every advantage."

"The anarachs don't scare me," I said. "I'm a prisoner to some extent already, in this body. We could use the ring. The risk is outweighed by the gain."

"Then I'll go along with the rest of you. General Paint?"

"I relish any opportunity to find myself surrounded by stone and earth again."

"Then it's decided," said Centaur. "After we settle in Jasper, we'll begin looking for an entrance into the underworld."

"If we can tolerate being near those men again, it's probable they'll inadvertently divulge it," I remarked.

"Or we could just shake it out of them," suggested General Paint.

"Let's sleep on it," said Centaur. "A plan will work itself out in the morning."

I paid extra attention to my surroundings that night.
Prudence or inevitability? I heard sounds outside the door. They
didn't sound human: small, scurrying feet; squeaks. The sounds
suddenly stopped. I looked at the door knob. It didn't move. Then
I saw some movement, but it wasn't at the door, but beneath it.
Four pink rats with sharp noses and beady eyes squeezed under the
door. When all were inside, the rats grew as they morphed into
humans. If I had been sleeping they would have robbed and/or
killed us in our sleep. They crept towards my companions without
making a sound. I clapped my stone hands together. The ratmen
jumped half their height into the air, almost hitting their heads on
the ceiling. If they heard anything it should have originated from a
stirring sleeper. I took them by surprise, completely. By the time
they recovered my companions had their arms around them.

"If they begin to change shape squeeze them like you're
making juice," I said.

"We were just going to take a few coins," pleaded one.

"And maybe those three stones," said another.

"And those weapons," said a third.

"We were just going to suffocate you a little," said the
fourth, "until you passed out."

"Not more?" asked Centaur.

"Accidents do happen sometimes."

"Silence is sometimes the best policy," I suggested to them.

"How do we enter the underworld beneath Jasper?" asked
Centaur.

"Emu won't let you pass through the Cheese Factory."

"You truly are an idiot, Scat. You told them where we live.
The Sheriff would have never searched such an obvious place."

"That's because the deputy we pay always leads him on the
wrong track, Dung."

"Why not tell them that we've dug a tunnel under the
bank?"

"Or that we're going to rob Gander when he goes on vacation next week."

"You four ought to hire yourselves out as town criers," Pulp commented.

"Are you going to kill us?"

"I think they'll be plenty of people to do that for us when you return to Jasper," said Centaur.

"You may wish to reconsider travelling to Blowing Sand," I said. "You could repent and join the Third Timers. You'll be completely concealed. None of your companions in crime will be able to recognize you."

It was still early, so we tied the changelings up outside our room. I watched them as my companions slept the remainder of the night. They were extraordinarily quiet. They must have been contemplating married life. Maybe the Church had a monastery, one requiring its residents to take an oath of silence.

Chapter 25

DONATING

In the morning we resumed our journey south. The ratmen headed north. They wore stoic expressions. In preparation for their nuptials?

The desert departed prior to arriving at the way station. The plains that replaced it became progressively verdant, transitioning into a jungle by midday. Pools of trapped water began to form beside the road, forcing it to climb onto a causeway. All manner of wildlife was seen: frogs, fish, lizards, storks, cranes, pelicans, even crocodiles. As we got closer to the sea, the pools transformed into an interconnected maze of waterways. Large homes on stilts began to appear on isolated islands. The land---what was left of it---varied trivially in elevation, just a meter above the water. If the sea rose, even modestly, the entire area would be underwater.

"Who would choose to live so far from Jasper?" asked Hornet. "Why aren't the people living out here more afraid?"

"The homes look like miniature castles," commented General Paint. "They're better protected than many of the villages we've passed through."

Jasper finally appeared, as a large walled island within a wide river. Walls didn't keep out all undesirables, but it did limit the number the city's police force had to deal with. Walls were also psychological. People who felt protected were more likely to retain their residency.

Jasper must have been a happening place: we could already hear music coming from it.

The road fell as it intersected the Naga River, continuing as a floating bridge. The uneven rocking motion was disorienting. Halfway across we fell into a rhythm. The one kay crossing began to feel more like a scenic walk than an obstacle course. We began to notice the wildlife: dolphins and swordfish, in particular, and fishermen in small fishing boats, catching fish and shrimp in their nets.

"We're going to eat well tonight," said Pulp.

"And inexpensively, I hope," said Centaur. "We're running out of money."

Near the city wall the bridge rose 20 meters, not only bringing the walkway up to the average elevation of the island, but creating a channel for ships to pass through. And there were plenty of ships. Most had large sails. A couple, none at all. What did they use for propulsion? Steam? Rowers? If so, how could they afford to pay so many people?

The island looked to be just over 500 hectares, one dimension being slightly larger than the other. The docks were 500 meters downstream from the bridge. A long ramp curved up the side of the city wall from the docks to an archway about the same elevation as the bridge's terminus at the city wall. The city was separated into five quarters---someone wasn't too good at math---each named after an animal class. The Reptilian Quarter was to the west, the Amphibian to the north, the Mammalian to the east, and the Avian to the south. The docks---outside the city walls---were called the Cod Quarter. The main thoroughfare was Equality Boulevard, which began at the terminus of the bridge we crossed. The unstable waters of the Naga River required travelers to hire a boat if they wished to reach the coast or road that shadowed it---technically, roads, the wide mouth of the delta making a continuous highway impossible. Ferries connected the thoroughfares, the crossings being neither inexpensive nor reliable. Too few people traveled by foot in this part of the Negative Frontier.

Jasper was known for two things: its diversity in mutants, and its love for music. There were entertainers everywhere, even beside the city gate. Two guards in rainbow uniforms greeted us enthusiastically. "Welcome to Jasper." Each wore five silver pins, each shaped like one of the animal representations of the five districts. They didn't wear armor, but they were armed, a dart pistol in an open holster at their side.

"How much do we owe you?" asked Centaur, frowning. Would we even have enough for a room tonight? If we were planning to travel by ship he had to have at least that much on him, wouldn't he?

The guards smiled. "You must not be from around here," one of them said. "Jasper earns its money by partnering with the entertainers. You can start paying your way by donating what you think is fair to these musicians."

The four who played were a diverse group. The lizard-like creature strung a simple three-string lute. The red and white striped bird struck a metal bowl with its beak. The monkey played an accordion. The frog's voice was its instrument, its croaking adding base to the ensemble. A metal cup was beside each of the musicians. Coppers---plus a silver or two---was in each.

"You have done quite well," Pulp commented.

The musicians stopped playing. The avian squawked, "We'd better. Only once every fortnight are we granted the gate."

Centaur placed a copper in each cup. The musicians stared at him. He placed another, and then a third. After draining his coppers, all 20 of them, the musicians returned to playing. "It would have been cheaper to pay the standard entry fee," Centaur grumbled.

"Entertainment doesn't come cheap," one of the guards agreed. The musicians were good, but not that good.

"How many more musicians are we going to have to pay?" The question was answered when we saw musicians lined up on both sides of Equality Boulevard.

"Maybe we can become musicians ourselves," Hornet suggested.

"We can't pay them all," Centaur muttered.

"Just look ahead and walk as fast as you can," suggested General Paint. "When I'm on patrol and I see a gold vein that's all I can do."

Centaur was firm in his abstinence. There were exceptions, but he never paid more than a copper. He cashed in a silver in preparation for his wavering reserve. He was able to bypass the homier musicians. The prettier ones, well, it had been awhile since he had a serious relationship with a woman. He missed his wife. If she didn't have that affair he wouldn't have been forced to kill her.

It was difficult to enjoy a particular musician with the conflicting sounds, so after a while we didn't try. Maybe one got used to it. Our circuits were overloaded.

Each district specialized in a specific type of business. The Reptilian Quarter in food, particularly of the raw variety. And I don't mean just sushi. The Amphibians were merchants. If you wanted to buy a luxury item, or a provision, that was the place to go. The Avians specialized in gambling and art. They liked their shiny objects. The Mammalian Quarter housed most of the humans. It specialized in spirituality and prostitution. The local Third Time Is A Charm Church was located there, but with a contingency no larger than Blowing Sand's. Mutant mammals were primarily laborers, many of them maintaining yards and homes. The Cod Quarter had a few restaurants and seafood processing plants, but a majority of its businesses were in the transportation industry. Jasper was the second busiest port in Limbo---after Capetown. Even if the city wasn't someone's final destination, many people stopped there for connecting voyages, or as part of a week-long cruise.

Most of the inns were along Equality Boulevard. A few of the more expensive ones towered over the city walls, providing views for their patrons. We couldn't afford them. We rented two rooms in the least expensive inn we felt safe. The rooms were small. Some people may have had difficulty sharing such a small space, but for those of us who spent the majority of their evenings in camp, it felt luxurious. We (meaning my companions) washed ourselves (their selves), and our (their) clothes, in the communal bathroom. We (they) had to pay a copper each for the hot water.

"At least the money's not going to those musicians," Centaur rationalized, more for his own benefit than ours. "Every time I give money to them it feels like I'm supporting their habit."

After putting on clean cloths (they, not me) we wandered down Equality Boulevard and some of its side streets. We (they) left our (their) packs and clothes (the ones that were drying) in our rooms, taking with us just our (their) weapons and (very light) wallets, the prior more for their safe-keeping than for our safety.

Like Blowing Sand, there was a significant police prescience. The difference: in Jasper there was also a lot of people, humans and mutants, running about, doing what they will. Nothing exactly got out of hand, but many of the things that went on wouldn't have been permitted in most cities.

The Mammalian Quarter not only had prostitution and gambling, but also a few good restaurants. On the way to one the innkeeper suggested, we were inundated with women on second story balconies exposing themselves. Gratuities were optional, but preferred, those dancing receiving the most coins. The restaurant the innkeeper suggested was called MOUNDS, the bottomless

119

buffet having topless servers.

We were given a dessert menu after the meal. What was described, and pictured, didn't involve food, not as a primary activity. My companions' interest, or lack, became a moot point: they couldn't afford any of the services.

Before returning to our inn, the RED PHOENIX, we asked where the Cheese Factory was. It was in the Reptilian Quarter, near the ramp leading down to the Cod Quarter. Understandable, considering some cheeses smelled as bad as fish.

It had been dark for an hour already, but we hadn't paid much attention to the decreased visibility due to how illuminated Equality Boulevard was. It was also the only street in Jasper that wasn't narrow and twisting. Away from it anything could be hiding in the shadows. We were comforted by our decision to retain our weapons.

We were left alone. Having a three meter tall gent as a companion does that. The majority of the Reptilian restaurants were along or near Equality Boulevard. Away from it were residences and food processing plants.

"I imagine some of the butchers reduced food cost by occasionally adding a lost tourist or two," said Hornet.

"Likely," I said. "Reptiles, no longer resembling humans in form or psyche, don't follow the human pact of not harming another human."

"There's the Cheese Factory," said Pulp.

"It's practically against the city wall," General Paint observed. "They must be aware of everything---and one---entering and leaving the city."

"Let's not get too close," said Centaur. "Not yet. It's best we don't have contact with anyone before we enter the place."

Two sharp-nosed, beady-eyed men left the building. They headed towards us, but turned down a side street before they saw us. "The best time to attack is at the end of a shift, when guards are tired and not paying attention," stated General Paint.

"So we just missed out," said Hornet. "When do you think

this shift is over?"

"Early to mid-morning," said Centaur.

"We could inform the authorities about their operation," I suggested. "If the rats are incarcerated it would be easier to find that subterranean entrance."

We returned to the Red Phoenix. I wished to return to flesh and blood one day, but consisting of sticks and stones had its advantages. My companions had this annoying habit of getting sleepy. The phoenix may rise again, but not they, not easily, not after going to bed a couple of hours earlier. Returning to the Cheese Factory so early in the morning was no longer believed to be the most suitable strategy. They all agreed, groggily, with my proposal to notify the authorities---then they went back to bed.

Chapter 26

DEPUTY

My companions woke---re-woke---an hour later, well past dawn. I was anxious to start the day. They wanted to ease into it. They insisted they eat breakfast before leaving the inn. How much of a person's life was wasted eating and sleeping? Many wouldn't consider it a waste, some even, a reason for living. As a drak I slept a lot, but that was commonsense. Draks consume considerable energy. If they were active 10 hours a day they would be constantly eating. That's another reason why we sleep as much as we do. Digesting an entire sheep or cow or elk or moose makes one sleepy. You try it.

We packed, then walked to the police station. It was just a couple of blocks down Equality Boulevard. We spoke to a deputy first of our discovery, then to the Sheriff. He invited us into his office.

"What I'm about to tell you," began the Sheriff, "must be kept confidential. Because you came to us with this information, I believe you are law-abiding citizens, as much as anyone can be who was given a life sentence. Having a Positive gent among you is a good indicator. I can perceive intent. That's one of the reasons why I hold this position---and retain my humanity. I'm aware of the rats, but I'm waiting for the right moment to arrest them. Their leader, Emu, is their mastermind. His presence is crucial."

"We heard that one of your deputies is on the take," Centaur informed him.

"He's a double agent. That's how we learned about their activities. Robbery is the tip of the iceberg. The key is Emu. No one knows what he looks like, not even my inside man. He's always masked, like he's married. We don't think he's even a rat. His stature is...wrong. He's larger and more confident."

"We can't be the only ones aware of their operation," I suggested. "For us to find out as much as we did in a couple of days...."

"You're sentient, aren't you?" asked the Sheriff.

"More so than most people."

"Would you like to work for me? If I had just one or two sentients I would learn 99% of what went on around here instead of 90. You might think that not knowing 10% was pretty good. A lot of bad can be concentrated in that 10%. Think of the hundredth of a percent of humanity that has been sentenced to Limbo."

"How much would you pay?" asked Centaur.

"Pardon me."

"How much would you pay Nimbus if he worked for you? Temporarily, of course. We wish to eventually leave Jasper."

"Deputies are paid a gold per week. That includes free lodging and food. I think I could go to two gold per week if I don't provide room and board."

"I believe bringing in Emu is worth more than two gold.

How about Nimbus working on a commission? If he helps you arrest Emu, then you pay him enough to provide passage across the Eastern Sea."

"Minimal lodging?"

"Just a small bunk each, and a couple of meals."

"Deal. With my government discount I think I can do it for three gold. But no boat if Emu isn't arrested."

"Agreed."

What have I become? Am I actually working for the cops?

The advantage I offered was my size, and that made me inconspicuous. It didn't hurt that most people thought of golems as toys.

I spent the next two days staking out the Cheese Factory. It was amazing the number of people that came and went from that building. A majority did legitimate business---who didn't like cheese? There were merchants, of course, and entertainers, tourists, even professionals, like healers and civic servants. A Wizard even entered once. He wore standard attire, the most prominent being a purple cloak, with the four symbols of elemental energy on the clasp at his neck. He had platinum hair, as did most Wizards who had been exposed to elem for a number of years. A red smudge on his bangs, also common with Wizards, marred the uniformity. There were many explanations for it. One rumor, that the majority of Wizards originally had red hair. Another, they employed red elem---elem fiero---on those rare occasions intimidation wasn't enough. The more elem fiero a Wizard consumed the larger the wound, as some called the patch. This particular Wizard had a fair amount of red relative to others I've seen, even more than the Wizard that had imprisoned me in my current body.

I got a bad feeling about this Wizard. Because of what happened to me, all Wizards brought a negative reaction, but this reaction was stronger than normal. Was it the way he presented himself? There was something different about him. Then I figured it out. Wizards normally didn't leave their penta shop. They kept to themselves, as if they were strangers in a foreign land. Their emporiums were like embassies: safe and familiar self-contained bastions. And this Wizard was social, not overly so, but he seemed to fit in with the locals.

The Wizard left the Cheese Factory. He was half a block away already. I almost lost him, being too absorbed in my contemplations. I followed him, but not too closely. Wizards had a way of becoming aware of those around them. He went directly to his emporium in the Amphibian Quarter. My draconian proclivities hadn't completely abandoned me. I involuntarily gawked at the beautiful things I saw through the shop windows along the way. I almost lost the Wizard again. His shop wasn't even on Equality Boulevard. It wasn't even in sight of it. Wizards didn't just set up shop to make a profit. They also did reconnaissance work. They didn't achieve their power just from their elemental manipulations. They knew what went on in the world. They also wanted their prescience to be known. They were arrogant, being on the top of the food chain. The Wizard I followed looked like he was trying to hide. How could he make any money if no one knew where his shop was? Passer-throughs bought as many penta as locals.

Something else was odd. It wasn't even midday and the Wizard was away from his shop. Wizards were always in them during standard business hours. It was considered unprofessional not to do so.

The emporium remained closed, hours after the Wizard entered. I watched it the remainder of the day. No one came into it or left it. Surveillance was the perfect activity for a golem: I never got tired or hungry.

I briefed the Sheriff. His response: "I guess I never knew enough about his kind to recognize the things you brought up. I must admit, I'm alarmed. I can contend with a crime syndicate, but not the most powerful group in the world. If the Wizard is involved with Emu and the rats, I pray he is acting on his own, not following the Tower's master plan."

"I presume you don't wish to raid the emporium."

"If I wish to retain my humanity. How many times will I be

124

killed if I trespass? Wizards consider their emporiums as more than a leased piece of land with a structure on it. Invading a building they occupy is like invading their tower.

"Whatever we do we need to do it soon. With a Wizard involved it won't take long for this to get out of hand. The longer we allow this to go on the more difficult it will be to clean it up. We may have to raid the Cheese Factory after all, with or without Emu. You're going to have to split your time between it and the emporium. Let me know---immediately---if the Wizard returns to the Cheese Factory. My counter agent may have to take more of a risk if Emu is to be caught in the raid."

I returned to my companions who hadn't been using their time as wisely as I. "I won more than I lost," General Paint announced. "It's like prospecting. You never know what windfall the next strike of the pick will bring."

"But you don't lose silver and gold in the process," I countered.

"Mining supplies aren't cheap."

"Isn't gambling considered to be chaotic?"

"Not if you have a system."

They didn't spend all their time gambling, but the last thing a person wanted to see after working all day were other people doing frivolous activities. Was I really supporting a family of five? It's about time I put them to work. "Don't plan on staying out all night tonight. You're getting up early." The toy had become a man. I was irritated, but felt great. The tumble had been substantial. Becoming a golem, I assumed I would never lead again, never again have responsibility and respect. The meek may not inherit Limbo, but they didn't have to grovel either.

I returned to the Sheriff, asking to speak to the counter agent. He happened to be in the police station so I was able to converse with him immediately. It wasn't too surprising why the rats believed he would spy for them. He looked like them. More than looked---he was actually one of them. Being as connected to the elements as I was, once I studied a mutational sub-species I could recognize the characteristics in others. I considered it to be a signature, not of an individual, but of an entire breed.

I pulled the Sheriff aside. "Are you aware this man is a rat? His appearance isn't a disguise. Maybe it's you who is being double-crossed."

"Of course he is. Do you think a disguise could transform someone into a rodent? Some people aren't content with the form Gaea gave them. Morality is the greatest determinant of future re-creations. We have substantial input in what we become."

Turning to the counter-agent, I asked him, "How often do you see Emu?"

"I've seen him five times in the two months I've been a member of his crew. I never know in advance when he will appear."

"Has anyone seen him outside the Cheese Factory?"

"I'm not aware of anyone even seeing him IN the Cheese Factory. He has always been below ground. He shows up without warning. He's upon us before we realize he's there."

Emu either already had the transport ring, or had a way of entering the rat lair other than through the Cheese Factory.

Chapter 27

BEETLEBACK

I woke my companions half an hour before daylight. They did a better job of waking than yesterday, there being no sensible delay to fall back on today.

General Paint shared his extensive military insight. "The key to an uncomplicated mission is to not make mistakes. The longer we drag it out the less likely it will be successful. Our elimination of the guards in the Cheese Factory must be precise. They mustn't be given an opportunity to warn their friends below."

"The deputies use tranquilizer darts," I informed him.

"They're going to have to be very quick-acting to prevent someone from calling out," said Centaur.

"They are. The neurotoxin relaxes muscles as the sedative knocks them out."

"You think the Sheriff will loan us a couple of those guns?"

"Certainly. We'll be doing the dirty work, and if we fail he can deny our connection to him."

"Pulp and I will do the shooting," General Paint stated.

"Wouldn't it be better if we all had guns?" Hornet questioned. "Twice the firepower."

"No."

"No?"

"An extremely weak tactical maneuver."

"I'm not that bad of a shot."

Centaur smiled. "You're not that good of one either. I no longer back away when you release an arrow, but I still grimace."

"I'm not that bad. I'm getting better. I've hit a few things."

"An extremely weak tactical maneuver," General Paint reiterated.

Centaur laughed.

Hornet looked sternly at him. "I'm not the only one General Paint thinks can't hit the broadside of a barn."

Without emotion, General Paint said, "If we were attacking a barn I would requisition four weapons."

Centaur laughed again. After he recovered, he said to the gent, "I didn't think trogs had a sense of humor."

"I don't believe they are aware either," Pulp responded.

Hornet still appeared agitated. "I may not be as accurate as Pulp or General Paint, but why turn down a couple of extra...."

"When you go to the dentist, do you wish there was a couple of extra people in your mouth?"

"Of course not. They would just get in the way."

Pulp smiled.

"If more than two come out?"

"If the commotion of an inaccurate artillery detail causes two dozen to come out?"

Getting into the Cheese Factory so we could shoot the two guards was the tricky part. This is where I came in. I knocked on the door, then stood there, motionless.

One of the rats examined the entry through a peephole. He saw me, unattended, with a note attached. He read it: "Sorry we couldn't return to Jasper to do our share of the work. We have collected great treasure, including this golem. We'll be back soon. Sincerely, Scat, Guano, Dung, and Offal."

"And you said they had run off. Open the door so we can have a better look at this thing. If we can get it do our work we can loaf."

I was carried inside. Why did they assume I would work for them if they didn't think I was capable of walking? Pulp and General Paint didn't dare shoot the rat yet, not with its companion safely inside to gather reinforcements. I was patient. The less bright someone was, the more likely they would become bored. It only took ten minutes for them to get frustrated with not being able to figure out how I worked. They wandered off.

I opened the door for my companions. Seconds later they shot the oblivious guards.

We found the stairs leading down to the basement, and from there a tunnel that led to the rat lair. Two dozen of them were still sleeping. It was impossible to tie them all up without waking some of them, so we slipped by, letting them sleep.

When they woke they would find the Cheese Factory unprotected. If the two men sleeping on the floor weren't killed on the spot, they would wish they were. What defense could they use: that a golem they carried in attacked them? I wasn't even still there, to validate that preposterous excuse.

"I'll find us another way out," General Paint promised. "There are catacombs in every direction. Some feel partially blocked, but the blockages are so insubstantial they're probably doors."

"Doors, down here?" Hornet questioned.

"A good indicator there are some places people don't want others to go," I said.

"Which way down?" asked Centaur.

"This way," said General Paint. "It drops quite a bit, then there's a barrier. There's a cluster of tunnels after that."

The descent was narrow, dark, and coarse. I already scraped my sticks-and-stones in a few places. I didn't regret being a golem so much when I thought about what the uneven walls and ceiling must have been doing to the flesh of my companions.

"We'd better go single-file," said Centaur. "General Paint, you'll act as SCOUT. Hornet and Pulp, you'll go next, as ART1 and 2. Ready your bows. In these close quarters we won't have much time to react. Nimbus and I will be PROC1 and 2. I don't think we'll be taken by surprise from behind, but the deeper we go into the bowels of the earth the more likely it could happen. We'll need a light source. Let's use a hooded lantern. That'll limit how much light we emit, and in which direction. That won't guarantee the light won't warn the anarachs and whatever else is down here, but it might reduce the odds, and prevent them from properly preparing for us."

"I should be in front," I stated. "I can see further than any of you, and General Paint will still be able to see over me."

"Agreed."

General Paint held a mace in one hand and the lantern in the other. He didn't need help seeing---trogs had excellent night vision---but he was near the front, and if Hornet or Pulp held it they would have been too encumbered to shoot their bows. Yes, Hornet was allowed to shoot again. And both felt more comfortable using something they were more familiar with.

We traveled slowly, our rate dependent on the radius of our illumination: the lantern revealed less than 10 meters of the twisting path in front of us. We didn't stop until a metal gate blocked our path a quarter later. The bars were spaced five sims apart. The crafting was poor, but metal was metal.

"I wish Pebble was here," said Centaur sadly. "He would have this gate open before we found the locking mechanism."

"I wonder if he is still with the terrans?" asked Hornet.

"We've come a long way since the four of us began this quest in the Bluewoods. Just two of us now. You think we'll see Stick again? None of us would have believed we would cross half of Limbo."

"With half of it still to cross."

"Ah, the good old days," I interrupted. "And they get older every minute we waste reminiscing. The longer we chat here the more likely we'll be noticed, if we haven't already. We have two choices. We can batter down the gate---not impossible, but it would take time. And the noise would attract a crowd. Or we could find a weakness in the structure and attempt to rupture it."

Hastily, the five of us scanned the iron, first visually, then physically. Near the bottom of the gate the metal was thin and not completely attached. We were able to push apart two of the bars and break off another. There still wasn't quite enough of a gap for a human to squeeze through, definitely not a gent, or a bulky trog. A golem could, though, and did.

A few meters past the gate was a chain. Quietly, I walked up to it and yanked it. It didn't move easily. Whatever pulley system was implemented wasn't very efficient. It made a lot of noise: metal scraping against metal, metal scraping against stone. Whoever built it, not only built it poorly, they didn't maintain it. My companions crawled beneath the gate as soon as it was high enough to do so. The space beyond the gate was wide enough for two to walk abreast, which we took advantage of. Centaur and General Paint were in front, each holding a shield, in addition to a one-handed weapon. Hornet and Pulp were behind them with bows cocked. I inherited the lantern.

A rumbling was heard ahead of us. Half-a-dozen meter tall hybrids of ant, spider, snake and human sprinted towards us. They rode on the backs of beetles. The beasts had huge mandibles that clicked. I couldn't decide what was more disturbing: the eerie sound they made, or what they might do to something caught between the pincers.

We stood our ground. It would have been impossible for all of us to squeeze back under the gate before they made contact. Hornet and Pulp each released an arrow. Both hit their marks. The two lead Anarachs---what else could they have been---were flung backwards off their steeds. Their beetles became confused. One bumped into the wall and stopped. The other kept coming. We flung ourselves against the wall. It rushed passed us, banging into the partially raised gate. The earth shook, bringing down pieces of stone and dust. It stopped where it hit, apparently unhurt, but remaining motionless.

Pulp, being an experienced bowman, was able to get off another arrow almost immediately. It also hit its mark. This time the rider was flung against the wall. The beetle behind it pinned it, until enough yellow goo was squeezed out of it to lubricate the wall to release it.

The riderless beetle persisted, its direction and speed not modified by losing its cargo. General Paint and Centaur braced themselves for the impact.

The other beetle from the second row, the one with a rider, struck General Paint. Its pincers were outstretched and extended, like harpoons. His armor deflected one of the pincers, but the other got him in the leg, just below the thigh, where his armor terminated. The impact would have sent him flying if he wasn't still attached. Instead, both the beetle and the trog shuddered from the collision of considerable masses.

Centaur had an easier time. The riderless beetle's pincers were closed. They acted more like a battering ram than a skewer. Centaur's shield, extended before him, took the brunt of the impact. He initially slid back, but his feet caught and he fell over. The beetle nearly trampled him, and Hornet, who was directly behind him. It hit the gate next to its companion. Its impact also caused some rocks and dust to fall---and the gate to partially detach from the ceiling and wall.

The last row of riders and beetles finally had their opportunity. The one behind the riderless beetle attacked General Paint. Hornet seized his sword as he stood back up, and together with Centaur, was able to fend off the beetle and its rider.

General Paint continued to fight, even with a beetle's mandible in his leg. The beetle was trying to free itself, moving its head back and forth, ripping the pincer through the trog's leg. Pulp considered releasing another arrow, but there were too many things in his way to get off a good shot. The wrenching pain in his leg finally became too much for General Paint. His intensity and attentiveness waned. The creature was able to bend down and bite the general on his neck. The trog slumped, providing a sufficient angle for it to finally rid itself of the unwanted encumbrance. With the trog no longer in his way, Pulp was able to skewer the anarach, two arrows entering it in rapid succession. It toppled off its steed.

The concentrated fighting had created a beetle jam. The anarach not yet involved in the action remained so.

After subduing his third opponent Pulp was able to work his way to General Paint and pull him back from the battle. The extra space created permitted Centaur and Hornet to flank the anarach who was attacking them. They finished it off. Without a rider to direct it, its mount stopped fighting.

The remaining anarach turned around and scuttled off.

I felt embarrassed for how useless I was in the battle. I was too small to fight, but I could have done something to help. I just stood there. I held the lantern---and raised the gate---but I should have done more.

We rushed to General Paint's aid. His leg looked like the main course at an all-you-can-eat buffet. If I had a stomach I would have emptied it. General Paint was conscious, but just barely. "Goooo...nowwww...don'tttt...aaaa...llowwww...themmm...toooo...reaaaady...aaaa...deeee...fensssse."

"Is that the injury making him sound that way?" asked Centaur.

"It's the anarach bite," I said. "Some toxins slow a person

132

down instead of killing them."

"Find the transport ring while you still can," said Hornet. "I'll look after him. I'm going to try to create one of Dinga's healing elixirs. I think the anarach may have inadvertently saved him by slowing down his metabolism enough to delay the complications of his injuries. GO!"

Chapter 28

PAPA

We left the lantern with Hornet. There was light ahead. If we needed more illumination we could light the other. Our degree of success depended on our haste. We ran with cautious abandon, I falling behind with my stubby, dowel legs.

The passage let to a manmade cavern, twice the size of a large two-story house. Seven unclothed rats---hybrids, not rodents---with brands on their backs served two anarachs---what looked to be---human arms. Pulp snapped. His laidback demeanor instantly became frantic. His eyes glazed. His breathing became labored and determined. His shot an anarach, then the other. In cold blood, yes, because they were probably cold-blooded. As soon as the act was consummated his demeanor reverted to what we had been accustomed to---except for his eyes, that became haunted.

The rats, instead of being ecstatic and generous, felt fear and a depression-induced dread.

"Cheer up," said Centaur. "We're freeing you."

"We'll be punished."

"Who'll take care of us?"

"Where is the ring?" I asked.

133

"Papa has a ring."

"He'll punish us."

"He'll take away our food."

"We'll punish you too." Pulp snapped again. He grabbed one of the malnourished rats. "And I'll do it right now."

"He'll punish us more."

Pulp hit the rat he held. He fell unconscious.

"Papa keeps the ring in his bedroom."

"Papa doesn't like us going in there."

"We'll show you the way, then we must return."

"Aunts and uncles may need to be fed or washed."

"Our sacrifice will be rewarded by Papa re-creating us in his image."

"Not too farfetched," Pulp forced out, his breathing not fully recovered. "Re-creations are influenced by strong beliefs."

Centaur looked concerned. "Pulp...."

"I'll...recuperate. I have recuperated."

"But for how long?"

"Until I'm re-created."

"This one episode can't have that much influence---to exceed years of Positive behavior and lifestyle."

"Two episodes."

"Two episodes can't have that much influence."

"There have also been sporadic...Negative... contemplations."

"Everyone has Negative thoughts occasionally."

"Not someone living in the Positive Frontier."

"We aren't in the Positive Frontier."

"That's what worries me the most. Must I be constantly inundated by Positivity to prevent this kind of behavior?"

"Better than an artificially induced moral stupor," I countered. "Shouldn't we be doing something about that anarach that fled?"

"When did you become so demanding?" asked Centaur.

"Just filling the void."

134

The anarach sleeping quarters were still partially occupied. The anarachs just lay there. They looked confused. Had they become so accustomed to their reputation, their intimidation allowing them to do what they wanted, their lack of DOING FOR THEMSELVES sapping their motivation?

We walked past them to the private room at the back of the small cavern. Inside was an anarach on a beetle, likely the one that had fled. A much larger anarach reclined on a sofa. The upholstery appeared to be rat skins. The frame, bones. "You are ssstrange ratsss?" it hissed through its serpentine head. "You have disssrupted usss. It will take many weeksss before the livesss you losssst are replenished. You feedsss usss, cleansss usss, digsss more tunnelsss. We don't eatsss you until many weeksss. If yousss behavesss you will be re-created asss usss. An honor to ssservesss Papa."

"You communicate well," I said.

"Learnsss ratsss language. Easssy. Sssimple. Othersss--- brothersss, sssisssstersss---think petsss, ssservantsss, foodsss should not be spoken to. You will watch and lisssten to Papa. It isss honor to ssservesss."

Centaur and Pulp had become quiet---and immobile. There was something about the creature's cadence and eyes. HE WAS HYPTNOTIZING THEM! He probably didn't even know he was doing it. It was a natural ability. No longer having a body of flesh, I wasn't affected. I saw the transport ring. It hung on a rat-gut strap around the large anarach's neck. Did it even know what it was, or just think it was pretty? The other anarachs began to cluster around the opening to their leader's chambers. Couldn't they have retained their stupor a few minutes longer? It was going to be more difficult escaping this place---much more difficult.

I clunked my stone hands together. Centaur and Pulp came out of their daze, but slowly. Then I set in motion something that was either going to get us killed, or allow us to escape. It was the only plan I thought had a possibility of succeeding. "How long ago were you re-creating into this form? When were you last human?"

"No humansss. Alwaysss anarach. Alwaysss anarach."

135

"If rats can mutate into anarachs isn't it possible that you have also mutated into an anarach from something else?"

"Alwaysss anarach." The leader began to mumble to itself. It looked confused. It continued to mumble to itself. Pulp had recovered enough to rip the ring from the anarach's neck. It didn't react, or appear to even notice.

We rushed past the anarachs huddled by the door. They were in as much of a daze as their leader. Eventually they'll break out of it. Rationalizing was easy when you made yourself your own god.

The rats still didn't want to leave. Centaur suggested we force them, for their own good.

"Let's just notify their kin that they still exist," Pulp countered. It pained his chaotic sensibilities to be forced to do anything---or for anyone else to be forced. "Knowledge of the servitude, and brutality, may be the deciding factor in them engaging the anarachs."

General Paint was already looking better. "I had enough elem aqua for two elixirs," Hornet explained. "I created one to heal flesh." The trog's leg was scared, but looked structurally sound. "I intended to create another to replenish energy---General Paint lost a lot of blood, and is still very weak---but he insisted I not waste the remaining elem on him."

"Snug within this stone womb my spirit is soaring," he said. "By the time we reach the surface I'll be completely recovered."

"The rats must be dealt with, and possibly Emu, and a Wizard," I said. I wasn't trying to be a pessimist. My intent was to undermine their overconfidence before they let their guard down. Our mission wasn't close to being completed.

"Weren't we going to find another route to the surface?" Hornet asked.

"Have you been able to navigate a detour, General Paint?"

"Not yet. The veins of emptiness remain muddled. I can almost feel my way to the surface. I get so close, then the tendrils get twisted, like a rope that ties itself into a knot."

"Your weakness has dulled your senses. If we are to discover an ulterior route we need you to be coherent."

"You must consume the replenishing elixir," Pulp insisted. "It may be days, even weeks before another necessity arises. We'll have time to replace it."

"It's agreed, then," said Centaur. Being a military man, General Paint knew how to take orders. He may not always agree with the decisions that were made, but he understood the chaos that would ensue if a consensus couldn't be reached, even a forced one.

Hornet mixed the elixir and gave it to General Paint. Its effects were instantaneous. There was a spark in the trog's eyes, a flush to his cheeks. He bounced up. His senses scanned. Like a blocked pipe that had suddenly freed itself of its obstruction, the tendrils extended with abandon, probing this way, then that way, until….. "I found it: a way out. It's so obvious. Just a few hundred meters this way, then a few hundred that way, then up here, then down there, then a kay or so that way." The twists and turns continued for half-a-minute. "Why couldn't I see it before?" His complex directions reminded me of the notation chess players used to record their moves. What was simplistic short-hand to them was a complex formula to those outside their world, especially when one looked at the jumble of letters and numbers in their entirety.

"Do you think the anarach king intentionally modified the rats' behavior, psychologically conditioning them?" asked Hornet. "So when they died they would be re-created into anarachs?"

"A psychological genetic engineering?" I responded. "Is it possible?" What the anarachs were doing reminded me of what the Wizard did to me. Could the two be connected? If I had a stomach it would have become queasy.

"If that theory proves true, and implemented, a vast army could be created," said General Paint. The concept was too disturbing to contemplate. The one thing that permitted Limbo to be livable was the localization of its seedier elements. The Frontiers didn't always exist, not until Gaea deemed it necessary to separate the morally extreme. A single species, with a substantial population could run rampant, conquering Limbo, then ruling with an iron fist. It would continue to grow as its victims were conditioned to not only behave, but appear, like them.

We were almost to the surface when a group of rats ambushed us. They had taken us by surprise so thoroughly that they pinned us before we could defend ourselves. Were we that immersed in our thoughts or had something been done to us to make us less aware of our environment? A masked man walked from the shadows to stand in front of us. "I believe you have something that belongs to me." He reached for the cord around Pulp's neck. He knew the location of the ring, even concealed beneath the gent's shirt. He tore it free, leaving a substantial mark on Pulp's neck. It looked like he had been hanged.

The masked man was in the process of placing the ring on his finger when I went berserk. From a spectator's point of view that's how it must have looked. It was actually quite calculated, in the second I thought of it. It's recommended if one is being kidnapped to not wait to attempt an escape. It must be done immediately. Once you are taken to a location of your kidnapper's choosing the odds of you ever freeing yourself is remote. Once it was decided that I had to make a move adrenaline overwhelmed me. Being no longer chemically based it shouldn't have happened. I was taken by surprise, but not as much as those who detained me. I broke free from the hands that held me, then cracked open the masked man's skull. The mask flew away from his face, revealing he was the Wizard. Not a complete surprise to me, but it stunned the rats. Their mysterious leader was dead...and a Wizard? They understood the ramifications of what had occurred and instantly fled.

"THE ANARACHS HAVE ENSLAVED SOME OF YOUR PEOPLE!" Pulp shouted at them. "FREE THEM NOW BEFORE THEY FORTIFY THEIR DEFENSES!" A moment later, he asked, "You think they will?"

"They're more likely on their way to join their friends in Blowing Sand," Centaur replied. "Bachelorhood is more exciting, but you'll live longer married."

Pulp turned towards me. "You are truly a marked man now. Killing a second Wizard, and this time with witnesses."

"And us as his accomplices," said Centaur. "We also need to flee. We must leave Jasper today, if possible."

"How about through the emporium?" Hornet suggested. "Assuming a tunnel leads to it."

"One passage does lead to it," stated General Paint.

"Isn't that the last place we want to go?" Centaur questioned.

"What's done is done," I said. "We can't get in much more trouble. I rod or a stone or two is fair compensation for the trouble the Wizard caused us."

We came to the door that would lead us up into the emporium. "WAIT!" I said as General Paint was on the precipice of pounding it in. "It's probably booby trapped."

"Another job Pebble would have been good at," said Centaur.

"We have a safe way in."

"The ring," said Pulp. "Has anyone ever activated a transport penta? Does anyone know how it works?"

"It can't work instantaneously, as soon as it's placed on a finger," I said. "If it did, the wearer would be popping all over the place."

"A specific place must be thought of," said Pulp.

"Did you ever actually go into the emporium?" Centaur asked me.

"That would have looked a bit odd, an unattended golem walking in."

"Then we have to think of another way."

"I'll try it blind," said Hornet. "You have all said I have this unnatural ability to not be harmed. It's about time we tested its limits. I'll visualize myself a stride beyond the door." He paused. "No one wants to talk me out of it?"

"We have confidence in your resistance," said Centaur. "And I haven't heard anyone come up with a better plan. It would be great to have an elemental arsenal, but healing stones are what we really need. Anything else would be a bonus."

Pulp handed Hornet the ring. "Aim for a few sims above the floor. It's safer to fall than to find your feet surrounded by wood or stone."

Hornet placed the ring on his right index finger. We gave him a lot of room. We weren't quite sure what was going to happen to him. Would he blow up? Would he be transported to where one of us was, and turn us both into stew?

Hornet faced the door, then closed his eyes. A moment later he vanished. We heard a stumble on the other side of the door and a shocked exclamation. "I'm safe. I'll return in a few minutes. It feels creepy sneaking around a Wizard's shop."

He returned with a handful of stones in one hand, and four rods in the other. He immediately removed the transport ring, afraid he may inadvertently travel to a random location. "I didn't find any rings. I didn't want to take too many things. The Wizard inheriting the shop may not notice...."

"Not very likely," said Pulp. "Wizards keep impeccable records."

"Oh well. It's not like they're going to ignore us killing one of their own."

"Why didn't you go out the door?" Centaur inquired.

"It never crossed my mind. I was so focused on collecting the elem and...escaping." Hornet placed the ring back on his finger and disappeared. He returned seconds later. "The door is also locked on the inside."

"We should have searched the Wizard more thoroughly," Centaur berated.

"Probably wouldn't have mattered," said Pulp. "Why use a key when you can instantaneously appear?"

"Good point."

We placed the score of stones in wallets, and the four rods in backpacks. The penta was dispersed among us, in case some of them were lost, or stolen. We didn't want to lose them all.

"Well, shall we break down this door or find an alternate

route to the surface?" asked Centaur.

"We could attempt transporting all of us," Pulp suggested.

"You haven't completely lost your Chaotic tendencies."

"It was Positivity that was waning. Chaos has always been a constant companion."

Hornet shook his head. "I'm willing to attempt it, but not in such an enclosed space. Outdoors maybe. In a field."

"That won't help us now," I stated.

"There's another exit two blocks away," General Paint shared.

Immersed in sunlight again we contemplated what to do. "We could sell one of the stones," suggested Centaur. "That ought to provide us enough gold to pay for passage across the sea."

"Won't that look a little incriminating?" Hornet commented. "After a Wizard is murdered someone wants to sell some penta."

"Considering how accessible the Wizard made himself it might be weeks before anyone knows he's dead."

"We need to see the Sheriff," I insisted.

"We don't need the money, now," said Centaur.

"I owe the Sheriff at least an edited version of what happened down there."

"You're not trying to be re-created in the West, are you?" asked Pulp.

Was I? Not intentionally. Did following through on a commitment, while inadvertently providing for the common good, make me a saint? I did what was necessary---and prudent.

Chapter 29

ANOTHER RELIABLE PERSON

My companions waited for me as I entered the police station. It was a task I had chosen to perform---and a precaution. They were accessories to the crime. A single arrest would be an inconvenience. All of us, a roadblock.

I told the Sheriff what I could without revealing too much about us. His response was surprising: "I'm going with you."

"Back to the scene of the crime?"

"On your journey---across the sea."

I didn't know how to respond. If the Sheriff was aware of our intentions---fully---I could understand. Who wouldn't want an opportunity to be free? But he didn't. Or did he? I didn't tell him, specifically, but there may have been subtle nuances. To solve cases he had to analyze data and process it. No, it couldn't be me, not in this form. Being emotionless had its advantages. Maybe he read one of the others. He spent little time with them, but an expert might be able to uncover what he needed in a few minutes.

How many more people are going to become aware of our mission? Were we being selfish not sharing? Was it wrong to escape while leaving others behind? Was it wrong to potentially free hundreds of thousands of criminals, many of them murders?

I understood why the common criminal wanted to escape, but why someone like the Sheriff? He not only had power here, but power that was well respected. He didn't have to steal or kill to achieve his position or retain it.

"Jasper isn't going to be the same after the Wizards discover what happened here," the Sheriff told me. "I believe the Wizard you killed wasn't involved with just the rats, but also the anarachs. I tell myself he was acting alone. If he was acting on the Tower's wishes our troubles, and all of Limbo's, are just beginning."

The Sheriff collected a few things, then left with me. "Aren't you going to inform your staff that you're leaving?" I asked.

"What isn't known can't be shared."

We joined my companions outside the police station. "The Sheriff has insisted he accompany us on our journey," I told them. They were too shocked to voice a complaint. There were advantages of having someone with us with his background, but that background was also the reason why it might not be worth the risk. We were becoming increasingly conspicuous---Pulp's prescience alone was like waving a flag while shooting fireworks into the air. It was becoming more difficult to get lost in the crowd, to reconstruct the portal anonymously.

"We need to stop by my apartment for a moment," spoke the Sheriff. Still stunned, my companions followed him blindly.

As we walked, the Sheriff shared a bit about himself: "My name is Cone Platinum Mountains. I sense you are shocked that I arrived in the Positive Frontier. Most people think I'm lying when I say it, to make myself more righteous or pious, so I haven't told anyone in a while."

"No one ever enters Limbo in the Frontiers," stated General Paint.

"No one I'm aware of, except me. I understand the antagonism. Some people try their entire life to be re-created in the Positive Frontier, and I'm born there. I regret not meeting any trogs while I was in the Platinum Mountains. Most of your kind keep to themselves underground. I knew some partials. You could say they raised me.

"I was a lawman before I came to Limbo. A good one, but sometimes I became zealous. The police brutality charge may have been fair, but the man got what he deserved: a life sentence for murdering two small children while attempting to steal their holograph machine was too lenient.

"After three years living in the Positive Frontier there wasn't enough excitement for me, or justification for my existence. I returned to police work after traveling to the Negative Frontier."

"Why would you wish to travel with us?" asked Hornet. "It has to be more than escaping what might happen here."

"I've contemplated leaving for a while. Police work---here---is becoming monotonous. If there was global law enforcement I would have already joined it."

"You could become an Octagonal Knights," Hornet suggested.

"There are too few and they strive for balance, not order. I think I might try my hand at being a nomadic private investigator."

"We have specific places in mind to travel," said Centaur.

"Anywhere different is fine with me. Once your journey becomes stale I may wish to part ways with you."

We all chuckled. "You're going to wish you were back in Jasper in a week," said Pulp. "You'll either have the time of your life with us, or become prematurely gray---which is saying something on planet with slow aging and a low life-expectancy."

"Have you considered we may not wish you to join us?" asked Centaur.

"I'm good at reading people. I feel you could use another reliable person. Anyone heading east should accept whatever help that is offered."

"What makes you think we're heading east?" East was a euphemism for the Negative Frontier. "Someone hiring a ship in Jasper might go anywhere. We could be heading south to the Liver Peninsula. Or even west. Gents and trogs don't spend a lot of time away from home."

"Men---and mutes---with stern countenances aren't heading west. Usually not south either, unless they're in route...to somewhere less desirable."

The Sheriff---just Cone now---like all public servants, didn't live in a particularly spacious home. He must have spent most of his time at work, because he sure didn't spend it doing any cleaning. He grabbed a few trail provisions and was off again. No longer believing violence was an acceptable tool to safeguard society, he carried two stun dart guns, holstered on a belt laden with extra darts.

We arrived at the Cod Quarter as a ship began unloading. A man, head to toe in platinum armor, with a concave octagon in gold on the chest, walked down the loading plank. "STICK!" Centaur sprinted to greet the Octagonal Knight. He clutched his shoulders. Stick looked sick. Centaur couldn't have squeezed him that hard.

The rest of us also greeted Stick, but not so severely. None of us believed we would see him again after he was burned to death by the orb. But Octagonal Knights, Defenders of the People, Proponents of Neutrality, couldn't die, could they?

"My body regenerated in the Octagonal Prism. I returned to Orneg as rapidly as I could. Where is Dinga?"

"A djinn transported her back to Berry. We thought it best she give birth in Neutrality," said Hornet.

"And she agreed with this?"

"In time."

Cone smiled. "A djinn and miraculous pregnancies."

"It's not too late to change your mind," Centaur reminded him.

"No hesitation. Just contemplating how interesting the next couple of weeks may be."

"You certainly won't be bored."

Centaur made introductions. "Sheriff Cone joined us... about a half-an-hour ago. He'll accompany us until something more intriguing comes along. Stick...."

"You never mentioned you knew an Octagonal Knight."

"We know a lot of people. Stick was part of our group until...."

"I was transported to the Octagonal Prism," Stick interjected.

"So it's true, Octagonal Knights aren't re-created when they die?" asked Cone.

"Technically we are on the precipice of death when we are transported."

145

"Will you be joining us?"

"Affairs of the Order take precedence, but none prevent me from contributing to the advancement of our mission."

"May the wicked beware."

"Octagonal Knights are Proponents of Neutrality."

"Of course, as is justice."

"But all that can wait. All I want to do, now, is be on dry land for the next couple of days, and sleep."

"How long until the ship to Glen Aqua departs?" Centaur asked Cone.

"About an hour."

"You have that long to recover."

"It takes a while to recuperate from regeneration," Stick explained. "I was sick the entire voyage."

"I lost a finger," said General Paint, showing his missing digit.

"And I nearly burned my arm off," said Pulp.

"They don't have much sympathy for you, my friend," said Cone.

"They'll change their minds if they are in front of me when I vomit. So we're heading south, not east?"

"Disappointment for us not heading deeper into the Negative Frontier?" Cone questioned. "What have I gotten myself in for?"

We hired passage on one of these ships without sails. The SEA CHARIOT, like most ships in the Eastern Sea, had a mutant crew. The locath were semi-aquatic. They were nearly as tall as humans, and retained many of their characteristics. Their hands and feet were webbed, but they were still able to grip objects and walk gracefully. Their staccato speech was mumbled, like someone speaking with a fat lip, but comprehensible with minor concentration. Their scales were golden. Their greatest distinguishing characteristic was their dorsal fin. It varied in color, size, and shape. They wore no clothing or ornamentation. They were mutated enough to not appear scandalous. The captain's green dorsal fin was slightly larger than his mates.

Translated from mumble speech, the captain said to us as we boarded, "Gold-nine. Each. Cabins. Three."

"It used to be a gold-five, and we can squeeze into two cabins," insisted Cone.

"Expenses. Increase. Cabin. People. Two. Comfort. More."

"Shouldn't we get a discount for the cabin with one occupant?"

"One. Eat. Meals. Two. Locations. Crew. Enter. No. Unsafe."

As promised, Cone paid for our passage---along with his own. He had plenty of money. He fought for the principle of not paying exorbitantly. Civic or personal funds, we felt it prudent not to pry.

Chapter 30

THUMP, KICK

It was late in the day when we left port. The lights of Jasper became noticeable as the sun began to dim. At first they were distinct points, but as we moved further from the city, they became one immense blob, like the granddaddy of all fireflies was flying a few meters above the jungle. As we moved away from the docks into the Naga River we became aware of the peculiar propulsion system. There hadn't been any sounds or rumbling like one hears when an engine is idling, but as soon as we began moving turbulence was felt below us, as water rushed out behind the ship.

Curiosity overwhelmed us. "Captain," spoke Hornet. "How does this ship move?"

"Expensive. Very. Fuel. Scarce. Charge. More. Or. Sails. Install."

The ship began to slow. The captain signaled one of his mates. Words were exchanged in locath speech: a full-on mumble fest without constraint. The mate disappeared down the ramp into the hull. Locath apparently don't maneuver well on stairs. There were none on the entire ship.

After we had left port and were safely in the shipping lane, the crew of the Sea Chariot spent a considerable portion of their time staying wet. This lubrication took two forms. First, they all carried spray bottles, which they constantly used to retain a perspiration-like glean on their hides. Second, they poured water onto the deck with buckets to keep their feet moist. It became disconcerting, initially, but we eventually became accustomed to it. It was no worse than the cacophony of a crowded city or the permeated staleness of a smoky bar.

The channel didn't always stay in the center of the river. When it moved to either side we could hear the sounds of the jungle. The shrieks and cackles were frightening enough onboard ship. What would they have been like on land?

The isolated mansions became more isolated the farther we got from Jasper. They became non-existent after a quarter.

It may have appeared like we were heading into oblivion when we left the Naga River and its surrounding jungle for the open seas, but we only felt relief.

With nothing left to see from the railing, we went below, to our cabins. Each room had one set of bunks with two lockers beneath the bottom bed. We opened portholes to relieve the stuffiness. The hallway was lit by those red glow-beetles the trogs used. Torches and lanterns weren't welcomed on a wooden ship.

The crew's quarters were at the far end of the hallway. Two washrooms, one for the crew, the other for the passengers, separated the wings. Water was available for washing, but it came out slowly, doubtlessly to discourage its waste. The toilet was a raised wooden platform near the washroom's porthole. The moon dappled sea was seen below when the lid was raised. Large rubbery leaves were provided as toilet paper.

Life became less messy when one didn't eat. After my companions completed their digestive cycle we returned to our cabins. There was a lock on each door, but they could have been broken by anyone of average strength. I shared a cabin with Cone. It would have been extremely boring for me to remain in that two by three meter space for two-and-a-half hours. Fortunately, Cone couldn't sleep. Not unexpected considering the changes he was experiencing. We at first just lay there, silently, then we discussed our philosophies, and politics, and our visions for the future.

"The Three won't be able to hold power much longer," Cone stated. He referred to the three ruling families of the Galactic Federation. "There are too many spur groups that no longer want to be subservient to them."

"The reason peace has held so long is that power has been concentrated in so few," I responded.

"No group can retain power forever. Idleness sets in. Bureaucracy bogs down efficiency. There is always somebody else who has more enthusiasm."

"Your lineage?"

"52-28-20."

"I'm 20-28-52. We're complete opposites."

"Our ancestors may not determine who we become, but they must have some influence."

"Did you hear that?" I was referring to a thump in the cabin next door. It was one of those our party didn't occupy. I hadn't seen anyone enter it.

"I think it came from below." The noises in the bottom of the ship, where the propulsion system was, intensified with our closer proximity. There were turbulent, inconsistent thrusts of motion, and sounds of sloshing water.

Before I could comment, Cone's backpack rose. It fell back down, barely missing me. "That definitely didn't come from below."

"You don't have any spirits angry at you, do you?"

149

Then we heard a thump in the cabin on the other side of us.

"Something is making its rounds. Spirits can't kill you, can they?" I asked.

"They can't attack you directly. But if they drop something heavy enough on you, you could become injured, even die."

"Why would a spirit haunt a ship? Wouldn't it become bored after a while? If it felt so trapped in life, why would it want to trap itself in a wooden box in the middle of the sea?"

"This is where it probably died. Spirits don't haunt randomly. It's reassuring, isn't it, that someone died here, not too long ago."

"It could have been here for a while, couldn't it?"

"Not too long. Spirits hold onto their partial existence with whatever residual energy that remains, which isn't much. They don't even have the strength to appear visible. When all of their energy expires, they die, completely. I think it's time to do a little snooping."

Cone climbed down from his bunk. He didn't put on his boots or his armor. Both were liabilities on the sea. I followed him out the cabin, then down the hallway. We heard another thump. This time it definitely came from below. We walked to the door blocking the ramp down to the hull. It wasn't locked, but there was a sign stating, "CREW ONLY." Cone opened the door quietly. The swirling sound of water became more intense. "KICK!" was heard over moans, and then a shriek.

We rushed down the ramp. The hull was open bow and stern. In the center of the floor was a trough of water. Two-dozen mer---human upper torsos and aquatic lower---kicked at the water below them. They were supported by wooden planks---which they were chained to---20 sims above the surface of the water. Two locath watched over them, one on each end of the hull. They held whips they weren't shy about using. One of the guards spent most of his time dodging a small levitating crate that incessantly crashed into him. The crate finally broke apart when it hit the ground. One of the boards rose up and began to strike the other locath.

The guard not currently being attacked noticed us and pleaded, "Passengers. Allowed. No."

The other guard said, "CAPTAIN! GET!" The captain appeared before we were able to contemplate whether to carry out the decree. He must have also heard the commotion. Two locath followed him.

"You. Up," spoke the captain to us. The spirit either wasn't comfortable with the competing commotion, or decided to haunt somewhere else. Crates and pieces of wood no longer flew through the air.

"You have slaves?" asked Cone.

"Servants. Indentured. Rainbow-Isles. Sells. Papers. Proof. Ramp. Climb. Unsafe. Warned. Hurt. You. Accuse. No. I."

"Slavery isn't illegal?" I asked Cone.

"Owning them isn't. Capturing them is. If a mutant is already a slave when he is bought, he is treated like a piece of real estate. Owners can't be held responsible for everything that has occurred on, or to, their property."

"Can anyone become a slave, then?"

"Any mutant. A human can't become a slave under any circumstances. It's difficult to even arrest a human or to detain him. You should see the paperwork: all that documentation."

Cone turned to the captain. "You should have posted a notification that your ship has been infested by spirits."

"Unknown. Departure. Until. Passengers. Panic. Escape. No. Land. Until."

"You could have returned to Jasper."

"Losses. Afford. Barely. Kicker. Lost. Another. Kickers. Speed. Slower. Kicker. Spirit. Life. Hate. Revenge."

A chorus of anguished yelps were heard from the propulsion channel. A black cloud of humanoid shape entered the hull from the forward opening. It attacked the mer closest to it. The slave collapsed. A much smaller black cloud began to form. The pair of clouds left together through the opening.

"Gaea. Thank. Aboard. Servants. Indentured," spoke the captain. "Wraith. Hunt. Cease. No. Capture. Soul. Until.

Servants. Insurance."

"Will it return?" Cone asked.

"Kays. Away. Soul. Another. Before. Extract. Time. Until. Builds. Attraction. Feek. Mer. Need. Two. More."

We returned to our cabin. The spirit didn't disturb us again. Either it had other people to haunt or it was as disturbed by the wraith as we were and was no longer in the mood to haunt. Cone finally fell asleep. He snored. Not having ears, it was easy to tune out.

Chapter 31

A CROSS

In the morning, we (meaning the flesh-and-bloods) ate breakfast in the galley: hard biscuits drizzled with fish gravy, and tea. The latter must have had some medicinal qualities, because it settled Stick's sea sickness. Cone and I shared what had happened during the evening.

"I thought it was a party," said Hornet. "I've heard that people on cruises can get carried away."

"We need to be careful," Centaur insisted. "We can't afford to buy Pulp and General Paint back if someone enslaves them."

"Now that's just being cheap," said Pulp.

"I assure you, the attempt will be their last," spoke General Paint, no uncertainty in his tone.

"You'll be safe, Pulp," said Cone. "How many people are stupid enough to enslave a gent?"

"You'll be surprised," I said, referring to what happened to me.

The 500 kay crossing was going to take two days. Shortly after moonbright we entered Neutrality. Leaving Orneg, it was unlikely a second wraith would attack us. We entered the Rainbow Isles an hour later: seven islands ranging in size from 10,000 hectares to over 100,000. Strange that slavery was centered in Neutrality. I guess people didn't own and sell slaves to be evil, just to make a little money.

Before sundim, we stopped at Kaleidoscope, the largest settlement in the Rainbow Isles. The tropical paradise would have been a much deserved holiday for us, if we didn't have to be careful who we ran into. If we didn't have any dangerous adversaries already, we certainly made some in Jasper. The captain and most of his crew left the ship for supplies. They returned with three crates and two mer.

Pulp was visibly upset. I wasn't too happy about the purchase either, but knew better than to make a scene. Our anonymity was precarious. If our---my---connection to the murder of two Wizards was revealed our mission would fail. Wizards were wise enough not to kill: they apprehended, they tortured, they confined, they prevented escape by re-creation. Incarceration infinitum, they called it. Sensory deprivation and restricting movement limits opportunities.

"What type of man steals the freedom from another?" asked Pulp after the Sea Chariot departed. "Taking a person's possessions, even his life, isn't as despicable, as unworthy of redemption."

To see Pulp so worked up---again, who could forget how he reacted to the anarachs' atrocities---was almost as disturbing as someone actually losing his freedom. It was so out of character for him. It was like someone had stolen his innocence. Will it be returned, or will he live his life trapped in a cell of involuntary events and responses?

The second night aboard ship was less exhilarating than the first. We were safe from the Dead in Neutrality. My cabin mate fell asleep immediately.

In the morning we weren't within sight of land, in any direction. What would it be like if we never saw land again? Would rocks and trees become a dream?

At midday we saw land again, south of us. Glen Agua was just a hamlet, but it was the only settlement within a hundred kays in any direction, bestowing it the significance of a village, possibly even a town. Why wasn't there another settlement near it? People live in areas of great commercial, economical, or environmental appeal. Milky Marsh had none of that. It was a water-logged brine grassland that made the Muckmoors look like a city park. The hamlet consisted of a dozen structures on stilts five meters above the swamp. A rudimentary boardwalk three meters lower followed the coastline for a 500 meters in both directions. From there, ladders led down to an often washed away coastal road that headed west to Cape Town, and east to Cedar View. A boardwalk, perpendicular to the first, sloped down to a floating dock. It had one mooring for a large ship, and two others for smaller craft. More weren't needed. Ships didn't dally in Glen Agua, including our own.

We and six other passengers disembarked. Two dozen crates were unloaded, and as many were loaded. The ship immediately left after that, an hour before sundim. Cognizant of the propulsion of the ship now, I noticed the water rushing into the front of the hull and exiting out the rear. I was determined to no longer feel sorry for myself. I may no longer be a drak, but I could walk about freely.

We spent the night in MOSQUITO MANSION, the hamlet's lone inn. It was a one-story structure with just four rooms. As with most hamlets the inn doubled as a general store. We wished to leave early the next day so we purchased trail rations and a couple of other things before turning in.

Mosquito Mansion was more than a colorful name, it was a promise. The rooms appeared to be sealed well, but somehow the insects found their way in. The canopy beds did come with mosquito netting, which kept the insects out physically, but not mentally. The buzzing was more annoying than lulling.

Leaving the safety of the netting was an act of bravery for my companions. The insects completely ignored me. The flesh and bloods spent more time slapping than they did dressing. After putting on their armor, their maneuverability lessened, which increased the success of the mosquitoes. Especially vulnerable was the back of their legs. They all had welts by the time we dropped down from the wooden platforms of Glen Agua.

Stepping onto the marshlands was like stepping onto a sponge. The grasses supported in spots, in others we sank to our knees in gunk---their knees, my waist. Walking was like having suction cups attached to our feet. They stuck to the ground with the initial lifting of our legs, but with extra effort the mud around them detached. We became tired while still within sight of the hamlet.

The mosquitoes continued to attack. The jerking motions we made in our attempt to keep them away made our movement even more demanding. "There has to be a way to keep the mosquitoes away," said Centaur.

"The inn had that ointment you declined to buy," Hornet reminded him.

"It smelled like urine."

"I believe that was its major ingredient," I said. "Urine has antiseptic properties that reduce itching."

"There has to be a ward we can create from one of those stones or rods," said Pulp.

We took a break on a small rise above the marsh. It reminded me of that last stand before I died and was re-created into a drak. I scanned our surroundings, expecting something to attack us as it did in Briar Valley.

The stones and rods were placed on a tarp. Five runes represented the contents of each penta: a wave, water, elem aqua; a mountain, air, elem aero; a tree, earth, elem terra; and a flame, fire, elem fiero. "GAEA ALMIGHTY!" Pulp exclaimed. "There's also one with a cross."

We backed away, like the penta was cursed. And to some

extent, it was. One of the stones contained black elem, elem essence---someone's soul.

"We must leave it," General Paint demanded.

"We mustn't allow it to be in a state of suspended existence forever," I insisted. "We must release it."

"Release it?" Hornet inquired. "Just let it randomly infuse itself into something nearby? Into a mosquito perhaps, or a blade of grass? What type of existence would we condemn it to?"

"What type of existence, indeed."

"I didn't mean...."

"What type of existence can a person expect to have being trapped in a jumble of sticks-and-stones? No, an apology isn't necessary. We don't always choose our condition, but it is OUR decision how we choose to live our life. A person can either mope after a tragic injustice or use it as motivation."

"So, the appropriate action appears to be inaction," said Centaur. "I don't like carrying around a soul any more than you do, General Paint, but I don't think I could leave it here, either. There may not be an acceptable vessel to release the soul into---here--- now---but we may find one in our travels."

"Could we place it into someone recently deceased, before the body begins to decay?" asked Hornet

"Bodies begin to decay immediately," said Cone. "I speak from experience."

"Maybe if we timed it just right," said Centaur. "But that would mean we were aware of an impending death."

"To kill to allow another to live?" questioned Stick. "I don't think I could permit that. Octagonal Knights believe in balancing, not intentionally disturbing in order to create a situation that needs re-balancing. That would be like a firefighter starting a fire so he has something to put out."

Returning to the original motive for stopping, we scanned our penta, determining which one would keep the mosquitoes away. "I believe this stone creates an air barrier," said Cone. "I've had to learn some of the rune combinations in conjunction with investigations. The barrier may not be strong enough to repel everything, but certainly insects. If no one objects, I'll be the guinea pig." He swallowed the stone. A moment later air pushed past us, as it fled Cone. We tested the boundary of the barrier. The air became heavy about seven meters out.

"You must have some natural affinity to elem," spoke Pulp. "I've seen people use similar penta with only two meters or so of effectiveness."

"How long will it last?" asked Hornet.

"It depends on the user. Since Cone's affinity is apparently on the strong end, I'll say it should last the remainder of the day."

"Does this mean all penta I use will be this effective?" asked Cone.

"Probably, but it may just mean that this combination of elem is highly compatible with your body chemistry or mental signature."

"So, if a person is re-created into another form their affinity to penta might increase or decrease?" asked Hornet.

"Possibly. It could be like allergies: it might come and go. My guess is that elemental affinity is attached to the soul. If so, it'll change modestly, or not at all, after re-creation."

We continued our journey south, towards Paradise, a large village in the Jasmine Jungle. From there we would be able to follow a road, making travel easier. It was going to take three days to get there, assuming no unexpected tribulations.

The marsh began to get drier the more distance we put between ourselves and the coast. The tall grasses continued for two hours, then became sparse. Our pace quickened. We travelled three times as far the last half of the day as we did the first. The mosquitoes were replaced with flies, enough of them to be a nuisance, too few to be bothersome.

My companions slept peacefully in the open air as I guarded camp. I heard what sounded like hyenas, and saw a couple of pairs of eyes glowing in the dark, but nothing came close enough to camp to warrant waking anyone.

Chapter 32

THORNS AND MOSS

We began moving again after eating dried fish and fruit. We intended to make up the distance we lost the day before in the muck of Milky Marsh. We were determined to hike until sundim. We still had 120 kilometers to go. Travelling 40 kilometers a day was possible, assuming we didn't have any obstructions in our path.

We saw some wildlife the second day: wildebeest, giraffes, zebras, elephants, even a pride of lions. All kept their distance. Did we look that formidable? We also encountered a couple of more exotic beasts, or fleasts, as I thought of them---floral beasts--- because they were more plant-like than animal. What was the likelihood that someone would be re-created into a plant? What morality warranted a return to life as vegetation?

The low-lying grass, sparse and cracked, persisted throughout the second day. Infrequently, a baobab tree would appear, one of those trees that looked like it was upside down, its branches looking like roots, the scarcity of leaves conserving moisture. There was also the occasional watering hole that was more mud than water. We carried enough water with us---we hoped. We chose to not top off our fresh supply with that thick brown stuff.

At one of the mud holes we found the skeleton of what we speculated to be a jackal. Part of it was submerged in the mud--- another reason not to drink from the pool. The vegetation around the pool looked half dead. One of the plants was covered in thorns. It looked like a rosebush in winter. It was attached to the pool, by vines. They were dried out and broken. If they had received moisture from the water at one time, they didn't any longer.

Cone followed the broken vines with his eyes, then his feet. He stepped on them intermittently to determine whether they continued to fracture. One step caused a different reaction. The bush began to shake. Dozens of thorns became miniature darts. Cone was pricked in several locations. The red dots rose, becoming bumps.

"HORNET!" shouted Centaur. "Find a healing stone. IMMEDIATETLY!"

Hornet flung off his backpack and began searching frantically for the proper penta. "There isn't one that cures diseases."

"Make one with your free elem," I suggested. We used most of it, but we had enough for one more elixir.

Hornet mixed the remaining four elem aqua with an elem fiero. He force fed it to Cone. The bumps had spread to most of his body, and grew---to more than a sim in diameter. A moment later the bumps stabilized, then gradually diminished. The skin remained stretched, causing him to appear elderly, with leprosy.

"I found a Flesh Healing stone," said Pulp. Cone had recovered enough to consume it without assistance. His loose skin tightened and darkened, from a dead polar to a pinkish tan.

"Curiosity can kill more than the cat," said Stick.

"You were the type of person as a kid who lit matches, and let them burn down to your fingers to see what happens, weren't you?" said Hornet. "And you probably put your finger in an electrical socket."

"You don't learn if you don't experiment," Cone replied. "I don't trust hearsay."

"Neither do lemmings," said Centaur. "Just because the guy in front of you fell to his death, and the one before him, doesn't mean you will."

Later in the day, a family of hedgehogs crossed the trail in front of us. They must have been paying too much attention to us, because a jackal was able to intercept them. It got a nasty surprise when it leapt at one. The quills pin-cushioned its paws. It yelped in a high-pitched voice and fled---attempted to. The hedgehogs twisted into balls and rolled over it. It must have been stabbed a hundred times. Hedgehogs preferred their meat to be tenderized. The feast was disturbing, but also mesmerizing.

"That might be a good experiment for you," Stick suggested.

"My psyche has been scarred," Cone responded. "I will now believe everything I see and hear. I will buy all the new and improved products."

"Don't change too much," Stick cautioned. "We'll be reentering the Negative Frontier tomorrow. Free thinkers balance the unexpected."

"How does Neuneg differ from Orneg or Chaneg?" asked Hornet. He was referring to the Neutral-Negative, Ordered-Negative, and the Chaotic-Negative Frontiers.

"As one might expect, the mutants re-created in it are a combination of those in the other two Negative Frontiers," said Pulp. "They don't do heinous things consistently, or act violently randomly. Or, if you're more of a glass half full guy, they are the perfection of evil."

"And the next sphere has to be in Neuneg, doesn't it?"

Cone was shocked. "We are risking our humanity to find a ball? Is it made of solid gold?"

We looked at one another. I shared with the Sheriff what happened underground, but not of our attempt to reconstruct a transport portal. It had to come out eventually, didn't it, if he was to remain a member of our group for an extended period of time? No one knew, for sure, how a person might react to such news. Will he assist us with greater determination, or hinder us? Was preventing someone from breaking out of prison so ingrained in him that he would do whatever was required to stop us, even to his own detriment?

"Should we tell him?" asked General Paint.

"He'll have to know eventually if he wishes to retain our company," said Centaur. "Any objections to telling him?" No one responded.

It was wiser to tell the truth than have him guess something worse about us. Having someone with a law enforcement background had its advantages, but the disadvantages...they became quite blatant at times.

In great detail we shared those aspects of our mission I had kept from him. Be it the right decision, or the wrong, it made time fly.

"Would following blindly, without asking too many questions, be that bad?" Cone asked himself after he took a moment to digest what was shared with him. "If a lemur doesn't voluntarily go over the cliff on its own, it's probably pushed by the lemur behind it. Being a cop most of my life, I don't approve of you attempting to escape. But if I was perfect myself I wouldn't have been sentenced to Limbo. I'll stay with you, and even assist you to the best of my ability, but I won't be leaving. Not only don't I deserve a place in free society, I believe my abilities can be best served on a planet inundated with criminals. What better perpetual challenge."

Our goal of 40 kilometers was reached, and then some. All that talking distracted us from our tedious task. We completely forgot about our aching feet and legs, and draining energy.

At camp we connected the spheres to update the location of the next one. We were relieved we did. We were slightly off track. It would have been much worse if we caught the deviation a day later. From where we were, we needed to head south-southeast, instead of due south. We also discovered that we were much closer to the sphere than previously believed. We had dreaded having to travel to the heart of Neuneg. The magnitude of the spheres' attraction to the next indicated we wouldn't have to travel that much farther, barely into the Negative Frontier.

Dread waning, spirits rose. If it wasn't getting dark we would have hiked another 10 kays before setting up camp.

The savannah had become lusher the last hour of hiking. We saw trees in the distance, no doubt the beginning of the Jasmine Jungle. Somewhere in there, Neuneg began. Was there a relationship between the jungle's abundance and evil? And the plains' scarcity and Neutrality? Perhaps it was just a coincidence.

Another night without incident. It was doubtful my watch assisted with that, but I still liked to think so. I woke everyone, quite forcibly, at moonbrighten. I've been up for...well, since I became a golem. The least they could do was get their sorry butts up at the crack of dawn. We broke camp after a quick bite. The enthusiasm of the previous night had evaporated. The oppressive jungle awaited.

The trees never became dense enough that we couldn't walk through them at a slightly slower than normal pace. The underbrush associated with healthy forests wasn't present. There must have been a deep aquifer that only large trees with long roots could reach.

The transition from Neutrality to Neutral Negative occurred midday. It was like we had put on sunglasses. Our surroundings became uniformly dim. If felt like the trees had closed in on us.

"I need a break from this gloom," General Paint commented.

"I thought trogs preferred the dark," said Pulp.

"Natural dark, yes, but this place is smothering. Being blind would be more soothing."

We sat beneath large oaks dripping in moss. The entire area, including the ground, was littered with the stuff, like the trees were shedding. The moss was black, or maybe that was just because of the lighting. There was no moisture in it at all, but it wasn't brittle like it was dried out. It felt rubbery and strong, like it was made of nylon. My companions ate lunch silently. Blank looks began to appear on their countenances. They stopped eating. We had to get out of here. Before I could devise a plan, a piercing, ancient female voice pierced the murkiness. "CHILDREN, COME HOME. DINNER'S READY!"

Chapter 33

TILLED AND SOWED

My companions broke out of their stupor, but they were no longer the people who entered it. There was an unworldly innocence about them. They appeared simultaneously frightened and excited. They felt both comforted and upset from the intrusion the voice represented. They began walking towards it, leaving everything that wasn't on their backs where it sat.

My curiosity compelled me to follow them, then I became concerned. Being coerced by something in the Negative Frontier rarely turned out well. "HOLD UP!" They didn't. "STOP!"

"It's time for dinner," spoke Centaur in a little boy's voice.

"You just ate."

"We'll get in trouble if we aren't home in time for dinner," said Hornet. The coercive curse must be powerful for someone with Gaea's Grace to also be effected. Not having the strength to detain them, all I could do was follow.

I smelled bread cooking. A clearing appeared. The source of the voice was in front of a wooden house in the center of a weed-choked field. The old woman standing there had skin like tree bark. It was dark and deeply creviced. She wore a dress that appeared to be weaved from corn husks. Her hair was green, not brilliantly so, like new growth, but dark, almost black, like rotting vegetation. She was barefoot. Her toenails were long, and as sharp as talons, as were her fingernails.

"Come in and eat," the hag insisted. A steaming loaf of bread and a crock of purple preserve was placed in the center of a table set for four. It gave me some comfort, she not knowing how many of us there were. She retrieved a stool and placed it in one corner of the table. She added a place setting and rearranged the others. She stared at me, looking puzzled. She broke out of her trance when my companions sat down and began tearing chunks out of the bread. Some of them dipped the pieces in the preserve. Others were too eager to supplement it. Bread and preserves flew everywhere.

"USE THE KNIFE AND SPOON!" the hag bellowed. The diners stopped eating. They looked like they were about to cry. "Please use the knife and spoon. You don't want to make a mess of Granny's house now do you?" The diners sat there hesitantly, then Pulp grabbed the knife with a fist and began attacking the bread like he was stabbing something. "Let granny do that for you. You might hurt yourself." She sliced the remainder of the bread, then placed the knife high on a shelf. "I forgot the beverage." She poured a purple liquid into the five glasses on the table. The food and drink were consumed in minutes.

"More?" asked Stick.

"After you do your chores. We'll have cookies in a bit." She showed them what to do. The field needed to be tilled, then sowed. The hag didn't have any equipment, so they had to get down on their knees and use their hands to break up the soil.

I had no idea how to breach the curse. I wandered into the jungle to think. Maybe one of their stones or rods would cure them. But which one? It wasn't that I didn't care to learn what combination of elem did what. It wasn't necessary. I had confidence in the others to do that. I had relied on others to do things for me for so long that the concept of existing on my own merit was foreign to me. I did well when I was a drak, but in that form little effort was required.

I smelled something sweet. I didn't smell it on the way to the hag's house. That meant I wasn't going in the direction that would lead me to my companions' packs. I looked up to orient myself to the sun's static position. It was too hazy to distinguish the orb. The entire sky appeared to be the source of light. It was one opaque, illuminated mass.

Being upset that I couldn't help my friends, maybe not even find my way back to them, or the black moss, I took comfort in the only thing I could. I sought the source of the fragrance. Was that why the forest was called the Jasmine Jungle? How could something made out of sticks and stones smell? I could also see and hear, and feel. Was my soul able to translate what I sensed into familiar stimuli?

A kaleidoscope of flowers covered a small patch of the forest floor. My senses were overloaded. Seeing and smelling them wasn't enough. I had to touch the petals. A vine dropped around my neck. It was tightened, then raised. If I consisted of flesh and blood I would have died, by either affixation or a broken neck. Instead, I was just trapped. The vine continued to pull me up. I was being drawn into an opening in the tree's trunk, like an insect captured by a frog's tongue, but in slow motion. The sappy saliva coated me. Once completely inside the orifice, the mouth closed. It was pitch black. The tree lurched. I was sucked down into its center. The tree rumbled, then I was purged. I landed with a thud 10 meters from the flowers.

"You could have been more cautious," spoke an extremely tall woman in a bikini. She helped me up. The brunette had bronze skin and was barefoot like the hag, but her toes were perfectly pedicured. She was a meter taller than Pulp.

"Thank you, madam. This is the first time I have been in the Jasmine Jungle, so I wasn't aware of its dangers."

"Obviously. First, your friends sit in memory moss. Then Tulip takes advantage of your friends' condition. And third---THIRD!---you walk up to a hangman's tree. The only thing that saved you was giving it indigestion."

"I have a habit of doing that. Are you my fourth mistake?"

"Am I going to harm you? No. Not today. I'm feeling a bit Neutral this month. Living on a boundary, one has mixed feelings and morals. And being a woman...doesn't stabilize things. Don't get me wrong, I enjoy these fluctuations. I just wish I had more control over them. But being a man would be worse. They become very set in their ways. Variety is the spice of life, and men prefer their world to be unseasoned.

"You have a gent in your party. Being part of the Brotherhood---THOSE SEXIST BRUTES!---I'm compelled to assist Pulp. He has always treated me well, and women remember these things. It will also require him to do a favor for me some day. I would settle for him promising to not change his mind and not vote for the Brotherhood to have a greater role in Limboan affairs. I prefer isolation, and ruling Limbo is contrary to that belief. I would prefer to save the favor for something more stimulating."

"Are we going to free my friends now?"

"Pulp and his male companions could use another day of humility. Also, if Tulip has her field sowed by then, she won't need anyone else to assist her until harvest. It's not so much that I object to others being detained. It's the search parties. Anxiety doesn't create a peaceful atmosphere, does it? Tulip eventually frees them. If she didn't she would have to feed and house them, or kill them. Both are too much work for her."

"What are we going to do for the rest of the day, then?"

"You may do what you wish. I'm returning home. I don't look the way I do staying out all night."

I followed the female gent. What else did I have to do? I would probably get more lost if I wandered off somewhere.

We traveled for half-an-hour. I expected the gent to swing from a vine or something, but she simply walked, twice as fast as a non-height-enhanced person would, but she walked. I had to practically jog to keep up with her, which wasn't easy on stone feet. Being as tall as she was, I thought she would have to consistently duck, but she never did, not even once. She knew instinctively which route to take through the unmarked woods. She exhibited flawless grace. She flowed through the jungle like she was gliding through air.

She suddenly stopped, looking at the ground, then up at the canopy. She snatched the bow that had been slung around her neck, then pulled out a three-meter long arrow from the quiver on her back. She placed its tail against the string and drew it back. The wood bent backwards, creaking gently. She looked up again. She smiled, then let the arrow fly. It struck something. That something fell from 25 meters. It landed with a splat on the ground five meters in front of us. It looked human, except its lower torso, which looked like a spider.   It reminded me of the anarachs. It's what they may have looked like if they hadn't lost all of their humanity.   If an unadulterated spider fell from that height, in proportion to its size, it would have walked away, completely unharmed. But a 50 kilo creature falling from seven stories…. Broken bones embedded a ruptured torso. A rustling was heard in the trees. Five more of the creatures dropped from translucent lines. After hitting the ground, the lines detached. They scurried away on their eight legs.

"The spidermen and I have this game we play. They try to capture me. They don't succeed. I kill one or more of them."

"Why do they continue?"

"Hope, or possibly stupidity. If they try often enough they feel the odds are in their favor. That premise doesn't hold true, of course. Can a human ever outrun a horse?"

"If the horse was in poor health?"

"Stand back." The gent cut a translucent line I hadn't noticed until I was a stride away with a dagger the size of a long sword. She backed up. A silk net fell where she had stood. She cut the net away from the lines that held it in place. She rolled it up and carried it. "It's good building material." She stopped at the spiderman's carcass, examined it, then dragged it off by one leg.

"Also building material?"

"Spidermen aren't the tastiest of creatures, but if the proper seasonings are used, they're not half bad."

The gent's home wasn't much more than a very tall hut. "You're not impressed, are you?" she spoke. "What would you expect from someone who walked around in her underwear? I like comfort and simplicity. Do you think a gent needs to live in a mansion to impress people?"

"I've known a couple living in large castles."

"Sometimes gents build large houses to compensate for

what little they have in other areas. A giant isn't always giant everywhere." The gent laughed so hard she nearly fell over, and her mounds nearly out of her top. "Some of us, I'm afraid, are." She adjusted herself. "What's cute at two meters isn't so cute at four. But a girl has to live with what she's re-created with."

The gent set the silk net, and her bow and quiver, down. She attached the spiderman carcass to the skewer above the fire pit with two of its legs. Using a flint, its striker, and kindling, she had a crackling fire going within seconds. "I usually wait for the fire to die down before I put the meat on. It cooks more uniformly that way, but I'm feeling hungry NOW." She sighed. "Before I was incarcerated I craved chocolate. What have I become? What have we all become?"

The gent returned to the silk net. She opened a lidded tub and slapped a muddy looking paste to the edges of a hole in her hut. She spread the netting over it. More mud was applied, this time directly to the netting.

"Can I do something to help, ah...."

"Jasmine. Thanks for the offer, hun, but I think I got it covered." She laughed, but more gently this time. She was pretty at times, when one could think of her as a person, and not as a hulking giant. It must be lonely for her. There were rumors that pretty girls never went on dates because guys were too intimidated to ask them---certainly a myth. Would a four-meter tall woman have it any easier? What romantic companions could she have? Other gents? How many of them were there on Limbo? Was Coal the closest? If he was the type of person who was available to court her it explained why she was alone.

"This entire jungle was named after you?" I asked her.

She had finished with the repairs on her hut and walked up to me. "A tribute of sorts. We are both big boned and messy." She washed off in a basin with water barely cleaner than the mud on her hands.

Was I any better off than Jasmine when I was a drak? I lived in a hole. My only friend was a rock. She didn't even have that.

Jasmine ate the spiderman as I watched. She ate the legs first, then began working on the torsos, alternating between the spider and the human. Juices covered her face and dripped down her body. She was covered by the time she finished.

Sundim arrived halfway through her meal. It was very dark in the jungle, except for where the coals still radiated. With the Frontiers being so far from the sun only a fraction of its illumination brightened an open landscape. Under a canopy it was completely dark. Being a golem, I could see in the infrared spectrum, perceiving the pulsating shadows heat sources radiated. Jasmine gave off more energy than the fire. She reclined on a mat, relaxed and glistening. I almost thought of her as a woman: memories of emotions. The luxury of spending time with a goddess reminded me of my friends spending this same night with a hag---the injustice.

"I'm going to clean up," said Jasmine. "Want to join me?"

Chapter 34

WATERSKIING

Jasmine must have also been able to see in the dark. Her movement through the jungle was swift and decisive. I began to smell sulphur. Heat illuminated the area in front of us. Waves of it billowed into the air. In the infrared spectrum it looked like a curtain of flames. Jasmine stopped at a pool of water. She set down her bow and quiver of arrows. She leaned down, then slowly lowered herself into the water. The liquid went up to her shoulders. She took off her top and bottom and twisted them. She moved them through the water, then twisted them again. After doing it a third time she placed them on the lip of the pool.

"The minerals in the hot spring not only clean, soothe, and invigorate me, but also my clothes. I wish you were made of flesh so you could enjoy this."

I jumped in---as much of a symbolic act as a physical one. It wasn't for the potential sensation: I didn't want to be prohibited from the attempt. The water was above my head. My stone parts weighed me down enough that I wasn't able to float back up to the surface. A large fleshy hand grabbed my stick arm. Jasmine twirled me around her. I skimmed the surface of the water like I was waterskiing. I HAD FUN! Not emotionally---I still didn't FEEL---the intellectual equivalent. Jasmine released me. I slid towards the shore. Jasmine laughed sweetly. Momentum carried me to the edge of the pool. I grabbed the lip and pulled myself out. I felt invigorated. How could sticks and stones be that affected by a pool of water? My arms were no longer singed black. Did the soot wash off? It felt like my wooden parts were regenerated. Was the water fused with elem, like Lizard Spring? Evidently so, but to even a greater degree. I could make a fortune. No, why would I squander the wonder and beauty of this place, and the people who use it?

Jasmine stood up. The infrared heat waves blunted her shape, but not so much that I couldn't tell she was a woman. Water droplets fell from her, looking like shooting stars. She climbed out of the water and dressed. Her clothes, no longer coming into contact with the water or her, had cooled. They showed up darkly on her, emphasizing what was covered---another emotional flashback.

On our return to Jasmine's hut she halted us. A deer was ahead, but that wasn't all. A crimson cloud floated towards it. The deer didn't move. The cloud surrounded it, like fog. The cloud grew and became brighter. It floated away from the animal. The deer crumbled to the ground, looking more like a pile of fur and bones than something that leaped through the woods just seconds ago. Jasmine shot an arrow that glowed white, at the cloud. The cloud burst apart in a pink brilliance. A liquid of similar color splashed onto the ground beneath it.

"What was that?" I asked.

"The deer's liquid. Crimson clouds absorb moisture. That pool consists of blood, bile, urine, all the bodily fluids that make up a majority of one's body."

"Couldn't it just come by when you had to go to the bathroom in the middle of the night?"

Jasmine laughed at my poor attempt at humor.

"What did you use to destroy it?" I asked. "It didn't look like a normal arrow."

"It wasn't. I call it a silver arrow, but it's not really made out of silver. A penta's worth of elem aero is fused into it. Elem aero isn't very prevalent in a jungle, so I must trade with someone who has it. Elem terra is. With supply being greater than demand I must trade three elem terra for one elem aero. It takes me a week or more to find enough to make the exchange."

"And a normal arrow wouldn't have worked on the crimson cloud?"

"Some of the stronger mutants can only be killed by elem-fused weapons. The majority live in the Negative Frontier."

"After my friends are freed we'll have to infuse some of our weapons. If a penta of elem is used every time a mutant is struck we're going to need quite a few."

"Not all mutants are as difficult to destroy as the crimson cloud. The less severely mutated, those closely resembling humans, are usually the easiest. Five elem are required to infuse a weapon, but only one is spent. Instead of constantly infusing a weapon with an additional elem, weapons can be super-charged, more than five elem being fused into them, the extras replacing the ones consumed."

I watched Jasmine as she slept in her hut. Could a person be more beautiful asleep than awake? I think it had to do with a person sleeping was less likely to contrast your perception of them. When someone is awake any minute flaw can contradict the perfection pedestal.

In the morning I followed Jasmine towards the hag's house. "Where did your friends begin to act strange?" she asked.

"I don't remember, that's why I stumbled upon you. Due west of the hag's house, I think. Less than a kay away."

Jasmine led me right to it. The packs were still there, as was the black moss. Small replicas of my friends were formed from the substance. "These dolls contain the memories of your friends. Gather them. We'll return for the packs."

My companions were working in the field again. It was almost ready for planting. They became frightened when they saw Jasmine.

"They must consume their own replica. If they eat another, that's when the confusion really begins. It's best I stay here, at the edge of the field. You feed them the moss." My friends were more curious of me than frightened. They were happy to eat anything given to them. They looked famished. At first they appeared to be confused, painfully so, then they were able to meld the two sets of memories.

The hag came out of her house. "GET BACK TO WORK!" As soon as she noticed Jasmine she became depressed.

"You could do the work yourself," Jasmine suggested, with an exaggerated smile.

"We could help you," said General Paint. "In a couple of more hours we should have all the plowing done for you." Why my friends helped the hag, I never fully understood. Did they think of her as a grandmother? They were forced to work for her, but as slave owners went, she wasn't that bad. Maybe it was because two of them were from the Positive Frontier. If they didn't do it, who would? Better they than an elderly woman, or another group of deceived travelers. Granny, as they still called her, gave them cookies as they left. She smiled, smoothing out her wrinkles.

Jasmine escorted us back to the packs. Frantically, my friends filled them, wanting to be away from the memory moss as quickly as possible. Going too fast at times, many items were poorly arranged, or didn't find their way into packs at all. Having to repack as often as they did, they would have been better served to pack in a more patient manner. Nevertheless, we were able to continue our journey within minutes.

"You're not going to say anything to me, Pulp?" questioned Jasmine.

"Thank you for freeing us. I guess you want my vote."

"You could spend some time with me."

"We have been detained too long already."

"Go then, so I will no longer depress you with my prescience. No, I'm not going to demand a debt. The wonderful time I spent with Nimbus makes up for the inconvenience of freeing you. Good bye, hun." She kissed me on my stone head. "Maybe you'll visit me again."

Paradise, Jasmine Jungle's largest settlement, was just two hours southwest of where my friends lost their memories. We entered Neutrality again, raising our spirits. When we reached the Scimitar River they soared even higher. A kay later we entered the village. Paradise was a relative term. We stayed at the MONKEY MANSION, an inn cleaner than the ground beside it, but barely. The food was nearly as hygienic. If harmful bacteria were present on Limbo my friends would have died from food poisoning. Instead, the food just tasted terrible.

We had two options upon reaching the Sabre Desert, the perceived location of the fourth sphere. We could travel through the jungle for another day, then travel two more through a prairie. Or we could travel by boat down the Scimitar River to Palm Desert. It was farther, but some of that time spent traveling would be at night, and we wouldn't have to do any walking until we reached the town. We unanimously chose the second option.

Chapter 35

WEAPONS

It took two days---and one night---to reach Palm Desert. The 140 kays consisted mainly of traveling through prairie, but the last 50 were drier. The first 20 of that was through a canyon. At times the walls were over 2000 meters high. There were occasional pockets of vegetation, where a stream dropped down to the river, but for the most part the narrow, intermittent shore beside the river was desolate. The Falchion River merged with the Scimitar from the west, at the end of the canyon. It appeared that it also flowed through a canyon for many kays. The towering peninsula between the two river canyons was called Island of the Gods. It was rumored that powerful mutants lived there, but no one knew first hand, even draks, who gave it a wide berth.

The river widened after it left the canyon. Isolated farms began to appear along its western bank.

Palm Desert was growing. Its population was still under 10,000, but barely. It was going to become a major city one day---soon. It was centered in an extensive oasis that had grown as a result of canals being built, fed by the Scimitar River. The plethora of water brought a flood of immigrants. Pools appeared everywhere, not just beside mansions and resorts. Being so close to the Negative Frontier, a defensive wall had begun, now that its population and tourist gold could support it. It was debated how far out into the desert it be built. City planners didn't want to limit growth, but the farther away it was from the center of the town, the more expensive it would be, and the longer it would take to complete. A compromise was reached. The eastern wall would be built three kays from the river, the northern and southern walls, to be determined at a later date. Due to land being readily available housing prices were reasonable. Sunport, to the south, along the Southern Sea, was bursting with nearly 50,000 inhabitants. Its local resources were overused, steadily increasing prices, making Palm Desert even more attractive.

We stayed in a three-room cottage with its own pool. The temperature reached 40 degrees, but with so little moister in the air, and soaking in our pool, we---meaning they, the flesh and bloods---were quite comfortable. It was almost too warm to sleep, but like a majority of the residences of Palm Desert, most of the cottage was below ground. There were also vents in the roof. Hot air did rise, and my companions eventually became comfortable.

Before they turned in for the night, the spheres were connected. They pointed due east. We could have saved a few kays by traveling in more of a southeasterly direction, but doing so would have prevented us from taking advantage of a river flowing in the direction we intended to go. "Back to walking tomorrow," said Centaur bluntly.

"And into heat without shade or water," added Hornet.

"Maybe we can find penta to help us," Pulp suggested.

We displayed our elemental stones and rods on one of the beds. There were fifteen stones remaining, and two rods----plus assorted elem in the four collection rods. "And the Transport Ring," said Hornet. He placed it beside the other items.

"Being out of gold," said Centaur, "these are the weapons available to us."

"And our brawn." General Paint dropped his mace on the bed for emphasis.

"And our brains," said Cone. "We can out reason our opponents. To demonstrate, I will reveal the function of these devices: Temperature, Wind, Electricity, Heal Flesh---two, Heal Disease---also two, one Heal Energy, an Enlarge, a Water, and a Solidify. That's it for the stones. One of the rods is a Solid Barrier, with three charges remaining. The other is an Air Barrier, with five charges."

"How about the one with elem essence in it?" asked Hornet.

"Having no experience with one of those I can only speculate. It's probably more a holding device than functional, activation releasing the spirit."

"We don't need to be geniuses to determine what stone to use," said Centaur.

"How do we know it won't get hotter instead of colder?" Cone questioned.

"Penta are attuned to their manipulators," said Pulp. "If the person consuming it wishes the temperature to cool, it likely will."

"I don't recommend using it until we really need it," I suggested. "The benefits may expire before we---you---need it the most.

"Jasmine fused elem into some of her arrows to make them more powerful. She said using weapons like that was the only way to destroy the most powerful mutants."

"Sounds plausible," stated Cone. "A weapon fused with elem being able to concentrate the elemental energy into a small, defined area, making it locally more powerful."

"Do we have enough elem remaining in the collection rods to fuse a weapon or two?" asked Stick.

"Let's check," said Hornet. He studied all four collection rods. "We're completely out of elem aqua and elem aero. And we have just three elem terra, and one elem fiero."

"Not enough to make even one penta," said Centaur.

"We could collect elem fiero tomorrow, on our way to the sphere," I suggested.

"How long would that take?" asked General Paint. "I would prefer not to spend any more time in the desert than is necessary. Trogs are accustomed to be surrounded by cool earth, not an oven."

"Could we break into a stone and separate its components?" asked Hornet.

"Not safely," I said.

"We must take the time to infuse at least one weapon,"

Centaur insisted. "If claiming the next sphere is any more difficult than the last one, we won't survive this time without some assistance."

In the morning we walked past the walls' construction site and headed into the desert. There wasn't a road in the direction we intended to go, so we had to bushwhack. Fortunately there weren't too many bushes to whack. The construction workers thought we were crazy. They gave us some advice. "Beware the death dogs. Their saliva is so toxic that as soon as it makes contact with your skin it will begin to rot away. You'll be living zombies before you return."

My fleshy companions held off using the Temperature stone---until midday. They had been sweating profusely, but you wouldn't have known it by looking at them. The air was so dry that perspiration evaporated immediately.

"We didn't bring enough water," stated Centaur, emptying the first of his two canteens.

"We have that Water stone if we become desperate," Hornet reminded him.

We set up camp after the Temperature stone expired. It wasn't sundim yet, but we had suffered enough heat for one day--- even me, because I had to listen to all the whining. The tents added some shade, and that some was enough for my friends to no longer feel miserable, just uncomfortable.

Being unaffected by the heat, I began searching for elem fiero. We found just one so far. I may not be thrilled with the body I inhabited, but I recognized its advantages. I found four more elem fiero before sundim. That would provide us with one extra to fuse into a weapon, giving it a second charge.

Now whose weapon should we infuse? The majority of us suggested Stick, since he had a superior weapon to begin with. Being the person who learned the procedure from Jasmine, I was the logical choice to attempt the fusing. It was actually quite simple: place the elem collector against the blade, then release, discharging the six elem---the five required, plus one extra---one at a time. Elem would travel through the metal like current, combining into a penta when a sufficient quantity was clustered. Well, maybe it wasn't that simple. The elem left the collector, but bounced off the metal, back into the collector.

"Let me see that sword," said Pulp. He examined the blade as his hand slid along its surface. His eyes grew. "It's already fused with elem, but to an extreme degree, like a ring. I can feel a two-way flow."

"That must be how my armor and sword were transported to the Octagonal Prism," said Stick. "As my body regenerated I began to remember things that never occurred---to me. They were group memories, of Octagonal Knights, past and present. I have more questions than answers. I wish I had stayed longer in the Prism so I might consult my brothers, but I was eager to return to you."

"Me too," said Centaur. "What other powers might Octagonal Knights possess you aren't aware of?"

It was decided that Centaur's weapon would be fused. He did as much of the grunt work---the hand-to-hand fighting---as Stick. And, as leader, he rarely received benefits himself, choosing to provision his colleagues. The elem fused into his sword easily. Centaur swung his weapon. "If feels nearly the same: same weight, same balance. It does tingle when I hold it, like there's a small electrical current flowing through it. Should I use another weapon, saving this one for when we really need it?"

"I don't believe it will discharge unless it needs to," I said. "For weak, non-elemental adversaries, it should function like a normal sword."

We camped on the Neutral side of the morality border. We needed one more relatively peaceful night before, what could be, our last battle in our present forms. The spheres indicated we were significantly closer to the next one. Precluding unforeseen events---which occurred on a daily basis on Limbo---we'll have it in our possession by the end of the day tomorrow.

Chapter 36

SCULPTURES

We broke camp early, while it was still dark. We were eager for this leg of our mission to be completed---and to have copious kays behind us before it got hot. The one upside to entering the Negative Frontier: the murkiness cooled things off. I felt sympathy for my companions, but I also got tired of them complaining. Get over it. Was I constantly complaining about my body consisting of sticks and stones?

The third hour of travel looked like the second, which looked like the first. Looking back on it, I wish I cherished those casual moments more. When the bustle finally hit it was unrelenting. Being made of sticks-and-stones I didn't become fatigued, not physically. Eventually, anything, even constant activity, becomes boring without deviation.

The death dogs attacked first. The haziness of Neutral Negativity reduced visibility to one-hundred meters. Substantial when one's taking a casual stroll, but it feels like point blank range when one's being charged. The cacti didn't help. Every hazy shape became a potential attacker. Worse, every potential attacker became a cactus. We couldn't analyze everything around us rapidly enough to provide sufficient time to react.

We had been warned: beware the death dogs. Eerie was the best way to describe the twin-echoing barks. They were close to being simultaneous---close but not---like someone trying to sing along who wasn't in sync, inconsistently falling a syllable behind.

The dogs that finally emerged from the haze were huge, about the size of two large dogs conjoined, which they essentially were. Two heads rested on their shoulders. As soon as one head

179

yelped, the other followed a fraction of a second later. There were only a dozen of them, but if felt like we were in a stampede, a stampede you could partially see, paces in front of you.

There was confusion in how to react. The haze limited our bow range. How many, if any, would we be able to eliminate before they were upon us? We had decided---beforehand---if we were attacked in the desert Hornet and Pulp would stand adjacent, with the rest of us protecting them as they released their arrows. They surprised us. With larger than normal targets, and near point-blank range, the two archers hit everything they shot at.

Focusing so much on the frontal attack, one of the death dogs snuck in a bite on Cone's calf. The Sheriff killed it, but not before it gave him that rotting flesh disease the construction workers spoke of. It was already beginning to consume him.

The dogs became distracted. The smell of fresh blood was too much for them. They began to savagely tear apart their fallen brethren, gorging on the raw meat.

The rotting disease had spread to Cone's knee. "Hand me a Heal Disease and a Heal Flesh," demanded Hornet, impatiently.

Cone lay on the ground. He began to panic. "It feels like ants are crawling up my leg, eating as they go." His eyes became big as perspiration beaded.

"Swallow both of these, immediately," said Hornet. "If the rot spreads to your organs you'll die before we can cure you."

Cone grimaced as he took the stones from his right hand and tried to swallow them. They became stuck. The heat and panicking had dried out his throat. He began to choke. Centaur was first to hand him a canteen. The stones became dislodged with the lubrication. The rot had made it to the top of his thighs. It stopped advancing, then began to recede. With both healing stones in his system, his leg healed quickly, nearly as fast as the rot had consumed it.

The death dogs had moved to their third carcass. Two remained. Would they be sated? We chose not to risk it. We pulled Cone up and left the area as quickly as his weakened state permitted.

A low-lying storm appeared on the horizon, which in current conditions remained 100 meters. It looked like fog, beginning a meter off the ground and rising just a handful of meters. Unlike fog, it was coal black with white veins branching through it. We believed it to be heading in our direction, but it veered off, towards the death dogs. Being as focused as they were on eating they hadn't become aware of it. High winds caused course sand to fly at us, scraping away the top layer of my companions' skin, polishing me. For a moment I forgot about the predicament we were in as I savored the exfoliate. When the storm was within 10 meters of the death dogs the white lattice within it brightened. A lightning bolt jumped from it to one of the dogs. A hurried twin yelp was all it got out before it fell on its side. The cloud enveloped the dog. A minute later it moved towards another dog. It ran off before it could be attacked. The fallen dog looked like the deer the crimson cloud had consumed. Instead of following the dog, and its companions, who also fled, the storm spread out, reducing its height to two meters to compensate. It moved through the battlefield, eradicating the blood from the ground, like a vacuum.

We traveled as far as Cone's endurance permitted: about 10 kays. We oriented ourselves again with respect to the next sphere. The spheres pointed down almost as much as to the east.

"It's about time we went somewhere I want to go," said General Paint.

"How would you suggest we get there?" asked Centaur. "Dig?"

"Or find some...thing to do the digging for us." I pointed at dozens of creatures entering and leaving a large burrow. My companions looked confused. I escorted them the 50 or so paces required for THEM to see. How was it possible for sticks and stones to be superior to flesh and bones? It must have been startling to them for these insect-like creatures to suddenly appear. They were slightly smaller than a centaur---the re-created hybrid, not my friend. Instead of the lower torso being a horse, it was a scorpion, and instead of hands, the skor, as we began to refer to them, had pincers. Their shells and skin were red, like freshly cooked lobster. Their eyes were without pupils---completely white---adding to their inhuman appearance.

Stick turned to face Centaur. "Well, fearless leader. Do we have a plan?"

"Look at the sand sculptures," I interjected. "Sophistication AND creativity. We may be able to reason with them."

"Do you wish to revise that statement," asked Cone. The skor used their sculptures for target practice. They struck the likenesses of desert inhabitants with their rear stingers.

"They still built them."

"Why destroy something you put so much effort into?" asked Hornet. "Wouldn't constructing a pillar be quicker?"

"They must consider it process art," said Pulp. "Sometimes artists produce art just to experience the creativity. After the piece is completed it is destroyed to guarantee its uniqueness, and the work that went into it."

"So, how is this going to help us?"

"We create a distraction," Cone suggested. "We build our own sand sculpture. They'll believe Gaea created it to reward or challenge them. This once in a lifetime divine event may draw the skor out, emptying their lair. Then we can sneak in and take the sphere."

"And walk back out before the skor finish studying the sculpture, or praying to it, or making love to it, or destroying it?" asked Hornet.

"We found another way out of that labyrinth below Jasper," stated General Paint. "With as many tunnels below as there is there has to be another exit."

"You don't know?"

"I can't extend my senses through the empty spaces until I'm in them."

"Could we enter through one of those other exits?"

"For me to recognize a burrow from above I would have to be directly above it."

"The longer we spend looking for a way down the more likely we'll meet another monster, or two or three," said Centaur.

"So what are we going to build?" asked Pulp.

Most people conceive God in their own image, so we constructed a large skor. It was crude, but that was the best we could do in an hour. We created some noise near the sculpture, then fled, circling around the burrow. If we were to enter it, it had to be done from a direction the skor weren't traveling. We heard an initial commotion, then a few minutes later even more commotion. It was apparent from the thundering thumping that most of the skor had abandoned their lair to investigate Gaea's gift.

Chapter 37

AMETHYST

We traveled single file into the burrow. General Paint, being able to see in dim light and sense underground passages, led. Stick and Centaur followed with their elem-infused weapons. Centaur had a lantern ready, if necessary. Hornet and Pulp had their bows drawn. Then came Cone. I was proc. I could see in the dark, and be less damaged by a sneak attack.

It felt unsettling walking into that wide opening in the earth. Were we voluntarily walking to our doom? Would a mouse so graciously walk into a cat's mouth?

After the first turn of the entry tunnel it became apparent we would need the lantern. It was also apparent we needed a trog. "There are seven levels," stated General Paint. "Each one deeper and less developed."

"Which makes the bottom level the penthouse?" asked

Pulp.

"Which is the most likely location of the sphere," said Cone. "Treasures are usually not kept by the common man. We must assume the skor haven't mutated far enough from humanity to no longer have a class system."

There were numerous forks. General Paint must have known where he was going, because he never back-tracked. Whenever we traveled down an obviously descending corridor our confidence in him strengthened. Those brief times we arose a few meters, it waned.

We met our first skor on the third level. It was killed before it comprehended what we were. It wasn't able to recognize a visitor as an invader this far into the city. As we descended two more levels we met another five skor, but each time singularly. Apparently, atheists didn't congregate. Or maybe they were the dreamers, so lost in their own world they were oblivious to what went on in their colony, or above it.

Skor art wasn't limited to sand sculptures. Most tunnel intersections had an elaborate carving raised on the wall. They became more detailed and larger the deeper we traveled into the earth. On the sixth level a drak was carved, confirming the most prominent living in the lowest levels.

Major opposition was ahead. An entire company greeted us at the bottom of the descent to the lowest level. The tight passage gave us the advantage, it being too narrow for more than two skor to fight us simultaneously. With Centaur and Stick in front, their shields and elementally infused weapons extended before them, and Hornet, Pulp, and Cone behind them, with their arrows and darts, we maintained a formidable defense. General Paint led the counterattack. Being significantly taller than the trog, Centaur and Stick were able to fight over him as the trog chopped midsections and clipped legs. There were close calls with stingers, but they came early, before we got into a rhythm with our fighting. The few stinger strikes that made contact did so on armor.

The accumulative skor casualties began to block the tunnel,

pushing pincers and stingers beyond their range. "Is there another way into the seventh level?" asked Centaur.

"This is it," General Paint replied. "After a modest lattice of galleries and small chambers the open spaces terminate."

"Are we positive the sphere is behind that pile of skor?" I asked.

Cautiously, the spheres were reconnected. Those not involved in the activity watched both directions intently. Fate having a gruesome sense of humor, we expected the seventh level skor would break through the carcass barrier about the time the skor on the surface returned to their burrow, trapping us in a crossfire. The spheres pointed towards the barrier, but also down, even more steeply than before.

"Are there any tunnels that lead below the city?" asked Centaur.

"From the level above us," said General Paint.

"Then we better get moving. I don't want to be trapped down here when the skor return in mass."

"If we seal this passage it will delay the skor from following us," I suggested.

"The Solid Barrier rod?" Cone inquired.

Hornet retrieved the rod.

"Let's confirm the runes," said Centaur. "The consequences of an error are more dire underground."

"There should be four trees and one mountain," stated Cone.

Hornet twisted the rod until he spotted the runes. "Confirmed." He looked at Centaur, who nodded. He pointed the rod at the pile of skor. A translucent material began to form around it. Seconds later it solidified into rock.

"That ought to hold them for a while," said Pulp.

General Paint led us back up to the sixth level. We heard a stampede above us. "They're returning," said Hornet.

"We're almost to the tunnel leading away from the city." General Paint led us back to the drak carving. This time we headed in the direction of its tail. The rumbling became louder. Voices

185

were also heard, insect-like, but deeper. They echoed through the tunnels.

"We should also seal off this route," suggested Cone.

"That will leave us with just one more charge in the rod," said Hornet.

"Let's do it," said Centaur. "Why save something we may never have the opportunity to use. The last thing I want to do after being re-created is to return here." The tunnel closed behind us.

The tunnel leading away from the skor colony looked like the others, initially, before morphing into a more natural looking passage.

"This could take a while," commented Pulp after a quarter of walking.

We took a break as we connected the spheres one more time. The distance away was about the same, but the angle of descent wasn't as great.

Centaur turned to General Paint. "Do you think you can guide us to it?"

"These catacombs go on for kays, more kays than my senses can extend. I can sense density voids, but not the things within them unless they are comparatively massive, and then I am only aware of them. I can't determine their shape."

"I don't like this, at all," Cone spoke out. "We knew what we were getting ourselves in for when we believed the skor had the sphere. I don't like surprises. That's why I set up that extensive spy network in Jasper. The deeper we go the more dangerous the things we find---confirmed by your adventure with the anarachs."

"So you suggest we give up?" Centaur inquired. "We stop looking for the spheres? We become content with our condition? We live the remainder of our lives on Limbo, mutating into inhuman oblivion?"

"Of course not. I'm just stated my unease with the situation. Call me lazy if you will, but I prefer doing things the easy way, in the least stressful manner. Sometimes we don't have the luxury. Apparently this is one of those occasions."

General Paint looked pensive as he extended his sensory tendrils. Enlightenment sparkled in his eyes. "I sense a cluster of manmade passages."

"All these spheres, so far, have been guarded by something. Someone has taken ownership and created obstacles to maintain their retention. What are the odds the one we're looking for is unclaimed---for the moment?"

"It at least gives us a place to start," said Centaur. "Time to head out. Double-file when we can. General Paint, would you do us the honor again."

The trog led us deeper into the bowels of the earth, the natural tunnels continuing for kays. We descended more than rose, but there were considerable occurrences of both. Like watching a pot of water attempt to boil, every time we checked the location of the sphere it was noticeably closer, but still not quite there. At least we weren't moving further away.

The lantern reflected off something that sparkled. The tunnel turned, heading away from it.

"We need to stop," I insisted. I headed in the direction of the sparkles. I believed my friends followed me more because of the lantern I carried than in any confidence they had in me. The sparkles returned. I entered a 20 meter wide cavern. Its walls were amethyst crystals. As I brought the lantern closer to them the gems shined brighter. What I had first thought of as fallen crystals began to move. I RECOGNIZED THAT THOUGHT PATTERN! A small drak, just five meters from nose to tail, looked up at me. I never heard of a drak being that small. When a person is first created into a drak they are relatively small, but not that small: ten meters, fifteen meters, but never five. Unlike gents who remain the same size throughout their life, draks grow as they age, about a meter every three years.

Instead of having scales the small drak's hide consisted of amethyst crystals. "You have a beautiful home," I said to it. "Almost as beautiful as you."

It at first appeared shy, then frightened, as my companions entered. They had completely blocked its escape. It opened its mouth. Expecting flames, or something just as deadly, we backed away. Instead, it began to wail---high pitched and piercing. The amethyst cavern began to shake, knocking lose some of the crystals from the ceiling. Many of them fractured when they hit the ground, creating sharp, jagged shards.

"Please stop," I pleaded. "We won't harm you."

It did stop. It looked embarrassed, like a child caught doing something wrong, that it just found out was wrong.

"How long have you been a drak?" I asked it. My friends stood by quietly, not moving. One abrupt shift of a leg or an arm could cause the siren to resume. They let me do the communicating---a wise decision. A drak without a sense of self could be truly dangerous, committing hazardous acts without being aware of it.

"Two days," it whispered

"We need to do something," I said. "But I'll return in a few days to help you."

"DON'T LEAVE ME! I'M SCARED!" It began to whimper, then shifted to that high-pitched wail. More ceiling fell and shattered as it hit.

"Okay, you can come with me. But you must do exactly as I say, especially when I tell you to be completely quiet. I know moving is awkward for you now, but try to move quietly."

"Do you think this is a good idea?" Pulp whispered to me.

"I think it would have followed us anyway. A drak could come in handy. I'll keep it in back with me. I'll try to keep it quiet. The noises drak make are more likely to scare adversaries away than draw them to us."

Chapter 38

DEATH BY OCTAGONAL KNIGHT

We intersected a man-made tunnel. The bored hole was concave on the sides, flat on the top and the bottom. It was three meters high, about four wide. Pulp's head didn't touch the ceiling, but it came close. A pair of parallel metal rails were imbedded in the ground, extending infinitely in both directions.

"We aren't below a major city, are we?" Hornet asked.

Centaur retrieved his map of Limbo from his pack and examined it. "Palm Desert is the closest city."

"I haven't heard of a transcontinental railway," Cone commented.

"Me neither," said Pulp.

"General Paint?" asked Centaur.

"Trogs don't concern themselves with the rest of the world."

"Time to reorient ourselves to the sphere," I stated. What were these tracks doing down here? I had a few hypotheses, none of them comforting. To conceal something like this would have taken extraordinary planning---and vigilance.

"We're going to have to go down it, aren't we?" Hornet enquired hesitantly after the spheres confirmed what I feared.

Centaur looked ahead towards the continuation of the natural passage. "Unless...." He turned towards the trog.

"It doesn't jog back around. There's a large cavern in the direction of the sphere."

"You wouldn't happen to know if the sphere is in the cavern."

"The sphere's displacement is inadequate, but there are larger objects I can perceive."

189

"How many?"

"At least a dozen."

"It makes circumventing the skor seem like child's play," Stick commented, wryly. "I think I remember something about these tracks."

"Something you learned while you were regenerating in the Octagonal Prism?" Centaur asked.

Stick nodded. "The problem is I remember the memory---there being a memory---but not the details. I should have stayed."

"And miss out on this?" said Pulp.

"The sooner we head out the sooner we find the sphere," said Centaur without much enthusiasm.

"What happens if a train comes?" asked Hornet.

"We get out of the way," Cone answered.

Hornet scanned the tunnel. "And if we can't?"

"Let's hope there's an alcove nearby...or enough space to cling tightly to a wall or the ground."

After two extremely stressful kays General Paint halted us. "The cavern's ahead, about 200 meters, on the right."

"Should we extinguish the lantern?" asked Hornet.

"And do what?" asked Cone. "Hold hands, with General Paint on one end and Nimbus on the other? It's less likely that whoever is in the cavern to see us, but with us stumbling around, they're certainly hear us."

"I'll go ahead, to see what's ahead," I volunteered. "No one notices me, even in the light."

It became easier to see once the distracting illumination was several paces behind me. Another manmade tunnel, this one without rails, was where the cavern was supposed to be. It terminated after 30 meters, into an immense cavity, further than I could see. Doors and windows were carved out of mushrooms, dozens of meters high. None of the structures were illuminated. No one was here. I turned around. There was light coming from the tunnel I entered. It was dim, but perceptible. If someone was here they wouldn't be caught unaware. I returned to my friends.

"A forest of mushrooms, large enough to be carved into homes, but abandoned?" Centaur summarized. "No sign of the sphere?"

"Not from where I stood. A thorough investigation would have taken longer, longer than I felt I should be away from you. There doesn't appear to be anyone here, but for how long?"

"We'll spread out once we enter the cave, splitting up into pairs. The sooner we find that sphere the sooner we can abandon this place. General Paint, have you found a way out yet, back to the surface?"

"I believe so. That natural passage extends beyond my senses, but there is movement in it---air flowing---that usually indicates   a link to the surface."

"There might be a more direct route," I suggested. "We could continue down this tunnel."

There was initially no response. Who in their right mind would suggest such a thing? But I wasn't in my right mind now, not since I became a jumble of sticks and stones.

Pulp began to laugh, initially a rumble, building to a chortle. A gent flailing hysterically was never a good thing. From a distance, it might be entertaining, but never up close. A three-meter wingspan flopping this way, then that way, has a tendency to topple all objects in its path.

After we picked ourselves up, Centaur asked, "You about done?"

He wasn't, not entirely. Small outbursts popped up over the next couple of minutes: aftershocks.

"I wasn't aware Nimbus had a sense of humor," he explained. "It was completely unexpected. Something I needed before...whatever awful thing is going to happen...happens." Pulp breathed in deeply and stretched. "I believe I'm ready for anything now."

But it wasn't a joke---a thought I chose not to express. Our morale was so fragile I didn't dare risk a relapse.

Pulp's mood didn't last. He stopped abruptly at the entrance to the connector. He scowled as he examined symbols etched in the stone, first visually, then tactically, to confirm what he was seeing. "They're arbol hieroglyphics," he stated.

"Don't arbols live in forests?" Hornet asked.

"Yes," Pulp replied without emotion.

"And in the Positive Frontier?"

"Yes."

"It isn't natural," stated General Paint. "Arbols have always lived in trees, trogs underground. GAEA, you don't think there could be some disorderly, destructive trogs living in the clouds, do you?"

"What could have caused these arbols to immigrate beneath the Negative Frontier?" asked Hornet.

"The underworld doesn't follow the same moral boundaries as the surface," I reminded him.

"Something is affecting them," said Hornet. "Could it be like what happened to Trogdom?"

"Pockets of immorality, infecting like a disease," General Paint grumbled. "If I find out who did this...."

"It could have been accidental," I stated. "There are naturally-occurring pockets of poisonous gases beneath the earth, aren't there?"

"I would feel better if someone did this, then I could do something about it."

"What do the symbols say?" asked Cone.

"Fungi Gardens," said Pulp. "It must be the name of this place."

"Nothing about an amber sphere?"

Pulp shook his head.

"How about a treasury?" asked General Paint.

"Or a museum?" asked Centaur.

"Nothing like that. There are some locations listed here, with numbers after them: Grim 241, Sunport 99, Dreadful 374, Jasper 552...."

"JASPER!?" Cone bellowed. "Someone built a subway tunnel below Jasper without me being aware of it?"

"There are a lot of other places listed, including Gulag and Kenwood."

"The Platinum Mountains?" General Paint asked.

Pulp shook his head.

"That doesn't mean construction hasn't begun," said Centaur.

"So that pocket of immortality near Trogdom may have been a byproduct of constructing this Limboan subway?"

"Which doesn't confirm it was intentional," I said.

"The immortality pocket, not the construction. I must return to Trogdom."

"And I to Jasper," said Cone.

"This is what I couldn't remember," said Stick. "There are tunnels beneath Gulag. The Octagonal Knights have monitored them for years."

"Monitored, but have done nothing about?" General Paint questioned.

"Stakeouts take time," Cone enlightened. "Months. Sometimes years."

"Do you know what's being done?" Centaur asked Stick.

Stick shook his head sadly. "I should have stayed longer."

"I think I understand now why these arbols are living underground, in particular, beneath the Negative Frontier," said Pulp. "It's the ultimate celebration of chaos---to counter expectation to detriment: from climbing high to burrowing below, from chaos to order. No bolder statement could be made than sacrificing your morality."

"It's not that simple," said an apathetically sinister voice in front of us. A man looking very much like Stick, but in black armor, entered the connector tunnel. The crystal drak began to whimper. I attempted to console it. Where the man's face should have been was just darkness, with a pair of glowing red eyes floating in the void.

On the brink of us attacking it said, "No. Only an Octagonal Knight can harm me, because that is what I once was. After leaving the order, I died and became this, a Death Knight. I became dissatisfied with my life. I thought of how much time I had wasted helping others. What had I done for myself? Being unsettled, I was partially re-created. I became one of the Dead. The only way I can be re-created properly is to die properly. With my long ties to the order, only an Octagonal Knight can aid me."

"So you wish me to kill you so you can be freed from the form you now hold?" asked Stick.

"I will fight back. My self-preservation is too great to consent to a token defense. And I'll be too happy to send you back to the Octagonal Prism. You won't want to leave your friends, will you? Any scratch I might make, any dent in the Octagonal armor, will bring me but fleeting joy. But there will be others. You are already my third."

The Death Knight, whatever honor he once had long exhausted, struck at Stick at the tail of his soliloquy. Stick barely blocked the attack. He had to rely on his more instinct-driven defenses as he recovered enough to develop his offense. Amateur battles usually last less than a minute, poor defense allowing initial strikes to cause critical damage. Knights fought slowly, their psyches more geared to defending than killing. The rest of us kept our distance. One stray sword strike could destroy us. Fatigue was beginning to set in, not for the Death Knight, because he was already partially dead, but for Stick. No one could sustain perpetual aerobic activity. He began to let his guard down. After being knocked down, the Death Knight went in for the kill. Stick surprised us all by standing up. He struck the Death Knight from behind as it swung down. The Death Knight fell. Stick struck it again. The Death Knight crumbled apart. Then the crumbles crumbled, until there was nothing left.

Stick fell to his knees. "I made him think I was spent," he said between gasps. "That last attack, though, tapped the last of my reserves."

Hornet gave him the Energy stone without asking for a consensus, or Stick's permission.

Chapter 39

BYE, BYE

"I guess there was at least one person here," said Pulp.

"You should have questioned him before killing him," I berated.

"I've never been very good at multi-tasking," Stick retorted. "I had my work cut out just staying alive. Returning to the Octagonal Prism---now---would have been a bit inconvenient."

"Shall we?" asked Centaur, rhetorically. "Whoever still lives here is apparently aware of us. Stealth is no longer required. The longer we delay the more time we give the residents to fortify their defenses."

Light appeared at the end of the connector.

"That's quite considerate of those subterranean arbols," said Cone.

Pulp grimaced. "They're not arbols," he insisted.

"What shall we call them then?"

"Fungols?" Hornet suggested. "Arbols are tree dwellers. That makes fungols fungal dwellers."

My companions were mesmerized by the fungal towers. There were two dozen of them, each about fifteen meters tall. Windows---without panes---were notched in the structures, as was a single door at their base.

A small sphere at the top of the cavern glowed faintly, giving off as much light as Limbo's artificial moon did in the Frontiers.

A sphere was atop a tapered pedestal. Déjà vu. We expected a floating orb to materialize and attack. Instead, a very pale bald man in a black robe appeared. He wore a ring on every finger, including his thumbs. Closer examination altered my

195

assessment of him. He remained bald, but taken to the extreme. Not only did his head have no hair, it had no skin or flesh. A skull with light glowing from its eye and nose sockets floated above the robe. What I had first believed to be a lack of pigmentation, was polished bone.

"You're late," it hissed at us. Black vapor blew out its mouth, like its breath was considerably warmer, or cooler, than the air surrounding it. "It was inevitable you would find the Amber Sphere. Citrine might be more accurate, but amber tastes better on the tip of my tongue." It laughed shallowly, choking out vapor in intermittent bursts. "It isn't the loss of time that bothers me. In this form I do not sleep or eat, defecate or respire. Or pass through time. I return to the time stream whenever I wish. It is the disrespect, the lack of consideration, that I find most offensive."

"We must have lost track of our appointment," Pulp responded.

"Destinies do not follow a schedule. It is the strength of the obligation that hastens the arrival."

"I assume you have a purpose in greeting us," said Centaur.

"I will take the three spheres. Because you will not allow me to, I will have to kill you. You believe the last two spheres will be even more difficult for you to obtain. The Emerald and the Sapphire were potentially the most difficult for me, because they were in the Positive Frontier. Now that you have brought them to me, and the Amethyst, all that remains is to acquire the Garnet from the trolls, and the Ruby from the dragon. The trolls are difficult to defeat, because of their regenerative powers, but Gaea has a way of balancing things out, doesn't she? Thorn, she is greedy. She will trade the Ruby Sphere for something she perceives as being more valuable. She will try to keep both. That will be her undoing."

"Did you destroy the fungols?" asked Pulp.

"They prefer to be called borals. They have moved on. In their attempt to quench their insatiable need to bore virgin stone, they have become quite the diggers."

General Paint exploded. "THEY DON'T DIG! THEY ESCAVATE! One must bore gently, finding just the right place to strike with your pick. Before a digger moves on he must take the time to cherish the curves of the stone, the intricacies of the ridges and the indentations. Trog tunnels may appear to be straight, but if you look closely you will notice the rough texture curving this way, then that way. They're like the coastline of a sea. On a map it looks smooth, but if you walk along its shore you discover that 10 kays are actually 30. The map's scale conceals the capes and coves. The...fungols---it's blasphemy to say that other name---not only don't recognize them, they destroy them, using one to fill in the other. Their tunnels are dead."

"Dead or alive, for someone with the wisdom to choose the middle ground, it matters not to me. What does, they have dug over 100 kays of tunnels this past month. It won't be long now. Not long at all."

The crystal drak had behaved well up to this point. But all this arguing was upsetting her. She began to shriek. The cavern shook, bringing down a chunk of rock. It hit one of the towers, toppling it. The shriek being directed at the lich---what else would you call something that transformed itself into one of the Dead---it received the brunt of the sonic wave. It was pushed back three meters. It recovered enough to put out one of its hands. A translucent barrier appeared. The sonic waves bounced off it, the ricochet knocking us down, including the drak. Being caught unaware we scrambled just to stay alive. Hornet frantically dropped the stones and rods in his possession in front of him. One of the rods landed awkwardly, bouncing back up. It landed on a pile of fallen ceiling stones. After a flash of light the pile of stones reformed. They (it) began to move. The lich, thinking it was coming towards him, raised an arm in its direction. A lightning bolt struck the rock. It shattered into dozens of pieces.

The newly created elemental had distracted the lich long enough for us to rush it. I brought my stone fists down upon it, hoping to do to it what I did to the two Wizards. They bounced off a concentration of energy, likely the mechanism that contained the lich's spirit. It reached out to me. My wooden pieces went up in flames. The stones they connected fell to the ground. My consciousness must have just been in my head, because my extremities no longer felt like they were part of me.

I sensed more than saw the battle around me. I don't believe the lich comprehended our determination. Did it really think we were going to allow it to kill us without substantial resistance, even after our first casualty? Being partially dead lessened one's appreciation of life, and that was the lich's weakness: its fatal flaw.

It was difficult for it to react to everything at once. As it missed hitting Hornet, General Paint swung at it with his mace. It froze the weapon. After it bounced off the lich's energy shield it shattered into a dozen pieces. The trog almost cried.

Stick was next to assault it. The lich knew of an Octagonal Knight's abilities, so it focused all its energy in keeping him away. It shot out a burst of air that knocked Stick back into the crystal drak, who had been too overcome with emotion to express herself any more.

The distraction was what Centaur needed. He dropped his shield. With the added strength and support of a second hand he swung his elem-infused blade at the lich. It melted slowly through the lich like a dull knife through cheese. As it finally penetrated the energy shield, a white heat vaporized the skeleton beneath the robe. The robe caught on fire. Like an empty bag put into a flame the flare-up was brilliant, but short-lived, the fuel being consumed almost instantaneously. A moment later another burst of light erupted, this time from the edge of the sword. What remained of the lich turned to ash.

My friends rushed to the one stone that remained of me. Hornet frantically searched through the stockpile of stones and rods. Concern transitioned to hope. "The Solidify stone?" he suggested.

"No, that would not bring back my wooden parts," I said. "Give it to the stone golem we have created. It might not be too late to heal it."

I sensed Hornet swallowing the stone, then directing the energy towards the broken rocks. The stones fused back together. The elemental fled without speaking. Whatever gratitude it may have felt was tempered with being cursed to inhabit a body of stone.

The crystal drak came up to me and licked my head. "What is your name?" I asked it.

"I don't have a name," it shyly whispered back.

"What was your name before you became a drak?"

It looked confused, then asked, "When are you going to be like you were before?"

"I'll never be like that again. I must give you a name: Crystal. I know it's redundant, but considering the state I'm in what can you expect? Do you like that name, Crystal?"

"It's a pretty name."

"Crystal Underworld. No, that sounds too sinister. What do we call where we found you?"

"It looked to me like inside a gigantic geode," said General Paint. "Like she was hatched from one of Gaea's eggs."

"Then Crystal Geode it is. I need you to promise you will take care of Crystal for me. She may be larger than you, but she is still a child. I have never heard of a child being sentenced to Limbo before."

"But….," Pulp began before I abruptly cut him off.

"I can't continue like this. I don't want to be a burden. One of you needs to destroy me. If it helps, you can strike me from behind, so you won't see my face."

"I can't," said Pulp. The others didn't even give me the courtesy of replying.

"Bye, bye," said Crystal as she flicked her tail at me, sending me into the cavern wall. I sensed chaos, then oblivion.

Chapter 40

VERTICAL

My senses returned to me. I was back in the Raspberry Mountains. AMBER! The once drak, now elemental, nudged up against me. "Yes, I'm happy to see you again too." MY VOICE! I opened my eyes. I was a drak again. Never dying as a drak, I was permitted to be re-created in that form again.

After recovering from the weakness associated with re-creation I tested my wings. Flying was like riding a bike. It came back to me immediately.

Something was different about me. I searched myself for that difference. My body morphed from a basically horizontal creature, to one that was essentially vertical. Most of the free atoms---inert, free-floating particles that are taken in or expelled to modify one's size---left me. Instead of being 50 meters long, I was now four. Instead of a tail and wings I had human arms and legs.

I tried to morph back and did. I tried different shapes, but the only two I could achieve were a drak and a human, about twice its normal height. A smile filled my currently human face. "Amber, I'm going to have to mentor a very young drak. I'll be back one day, but I may make a side trip first."

*** This concludes book 4 of the Limbo Chronicles. ***

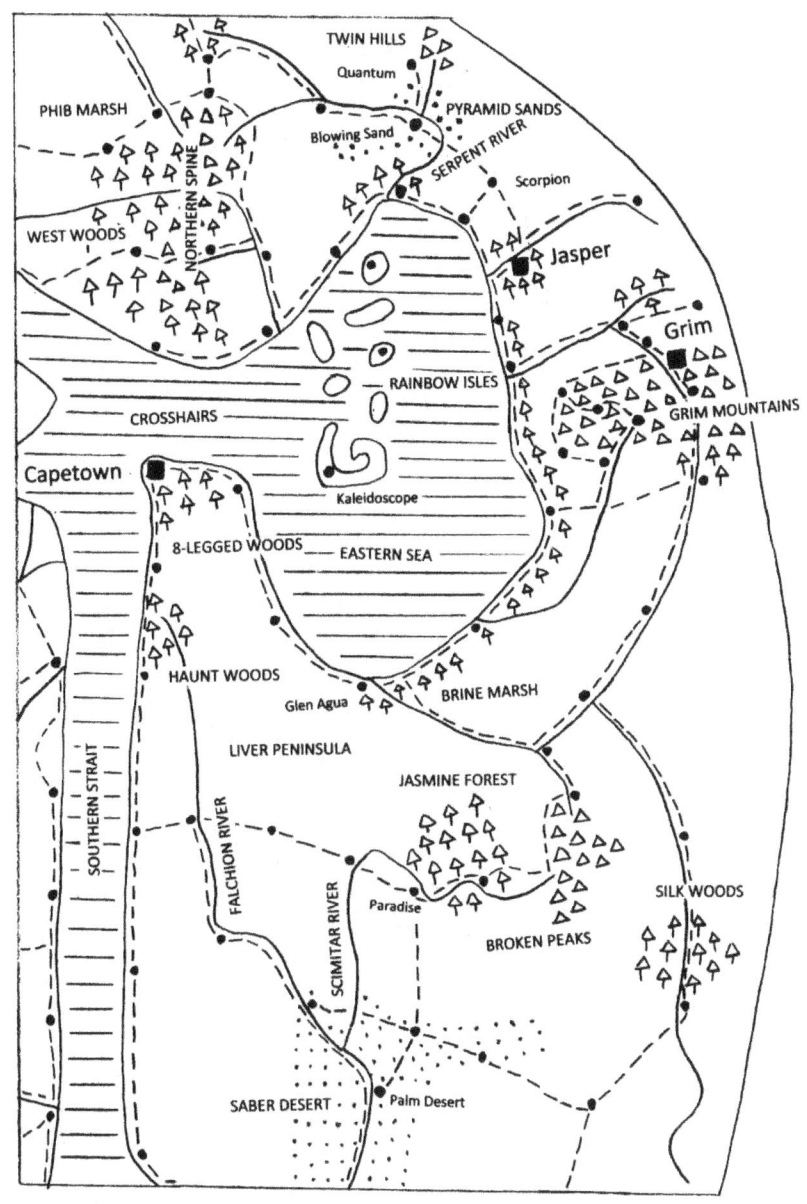